THE HOUSE THAT
Bethany
BUILT

BY
MARILYN TURNER

THE HOUSE THAT

Bethany

BUILT

United States Copyright Office

© 2017, The House that Bethany Built

Author: Marilyn Turner

Email: mlltnhim@gmail.com

Published by Anointed Fire™ House

Cover Design by Gail Jacques Designs

Website: www.anointedfirehouse.com

The stories in this book are fictional. Names, characters, businesses, places, events and incidents are either the products of the author's imagination or used in a fictitious manner. Any resemblance to actual persons, living or dead, or actual events is purely coincidental.

ISBN-13: 978-0-692-94512-4

This book is dedicated to...
Anyone who has suffered the loss of a loved one and
anyone who may be struggling with grief.

To those who may not have perfect families and to those
who struggle to find peace.

To those who have faith in God, to those who may be
struggling to find their way back to God. May you be
forever firm in faith. May you find your way to joy and
gratitude!
May He complete you, confirm, strengthen and establish
you.

May He make you what you ought to be.
I Peter 5:10

Table of Contents

Foreword

As an Editor and Publisher, I have seen my fair
share of Christian fiction books, but I can
honestly say that I have not come across one that
is as masterfully written as *The House that Bethany
Built*. Marilyn Love Turner is a multi-talented
woman who may have left the acting scene, but
the actress, comedian and writer in her is very
much alive and well.

The House that Bethany Built is as brilliant,
thought-provoking and hilarious as it is
revelatory. Bethany is an intelligent woman who
has allowed pain to reduce her to a life of
promiscuity, hatred and self-destruction. She has
everything that most people could ever dream of,
but her anger towards God has blinded her to this
fact and caused her life to become nothing short
of a nightmare.

The characters in this book bring their own
engaging (and memorable) personalities, all of
which come together to create an explosion of
laughter, joy, and love. The author took her time

to craft each personality, ensuring that no personality goes unnoticed. You will learn, laugh, cry and rejoice as Mrs. Turner gives you a life-changing tour of *The House that Bethany Built.*

—Tiffany Buckner
Author, Wise Her Still
Founder of Anointed Fire

Acknowledgments

My list of Gratitude is as follows ...

With Special thanks to:

The members of New Hope Int'l Ministries: I love you. Thank you for all that you do and for your prayer support and love. I Thank God for you.

My family: I'm so very grateful for your unconditional love. Thank you!

My editor and publisher: Ms. Tiffany Buckner. You are awesome!

My cover designer: Gail Jacques of Gail Jacques Designs. Thank you for creating such a special book cover for this story.

My loving and supportive husband: Apostle Charles Turner III. You make my world go round. I love you and I'm grateful for the husband, friend and lover you are to me.

Lastly and most importantly, Thank you to God, the Father, God, the Son and God Holy Spirit. You are my everything! I'm grateful that you saw fit to give me this new life!

BETHANY

Aramaic ~ beth 'anya

Biblical Meaning:
"House of Misery" or "Poor House"

From Wikipedia, the free encyclopedia

'The House of Song, the house of affliction'

Hitchcock's Bible Names Dictionary

Chapter One

BETHANY ON THE PROWL

Bethany masterfully whips her white Mercedes Sedan into the tight parking space as another driver in a badly dented Honda violently honks her horn, yells obscenities and finally speeds off to look for the next available parking spot. Sandy Leach, who's sitting in the passenger's seat next to Bethany begins to laugh as she compliments her friend on her aggressive driving skills. "Bethany, girl you get away with this just about every week. Personally, I don't know how you can find the nerve to blatantly steal someone's parking spot right in front of their face."

Bethany snaps back in a matter of fact tone, "Well, technically, it wasn't her parking spot; there is a such thing as first come, first served." Sandy chuckles, "Yeah, but Bethany, she was here first." Bethany quickly counters, "She might have been here first, but who parked first?" They both cut a laugh as Bethany turns the engine off. Then, like clockwork, she flips down the visor mirror, stretches towards the backseat, reaches inside her handbag and pulls out her makeup bag.

From the lit mirror, Bethany's over-sized almond shaped eyes pierce back at her as she begins to touch up her makeup. Like a mood ring reacting to a person's body temperature, the dim light illuminates her iris and reveals her mood. To check out her makeup, she slightly tilts her head and instantly, her hazel eyes change from a light brown to a cool green, appropriate to her calm and collected demeanor.

In contrast, is a "turned- up" Sandy. Bethany's friend glares out of the car window as she speaks to her, "Don't get me wrong, Bethany. I appreciate your aggressive driving, otherwise, we would be all night looking for a parking spot." She pauses for a moment to watch all the people in the parking lot migrating to the soon to be long line. "This place is on jam and I'm glad we don't have to stand in line."

The people are gathering to enter the hottest spot in town: Chaney's Banquet Bar and Lounge. It's lady's night at this 70's themed nightclub. In the line are patrons dressed in flamboyant 70's outfits, platform shoes, big hats and Afro wigs.

Sandy notices that Bethany is staring into the mirror as if she's fallen into some kind of trance. For a brief moment, Sandy gets a glimpse of her friend's loneliness and sadness. However, just as quickly as the secrets of Bethany's heart are revealed, they disappear and Sandy returns to her state of denial. She rushes her friend. "Come on, Bethany; you look fine! Quit primping."

Sandy raises both hands above her head and begins to snap her fingers and move her hips to the rhythm of an imaginary song. "I'm ready for the loud music, watered down drinks, and sweating on the dance floor. I'm gonna dance with a whole lot of Mr. Wrongs all night long."

But Bethany is not moved by her friend's eagerness. Instead, she casually runs her fingers through her tresses of long curls, which highlight her high cheek bones and flawless caramel skin. She plays with her dark curls for just a moment. After that, she touches up her full lips with red lipstick and flips up the visor mirror. Without saying a word to her friend, she grabs her handbag off the back seat, slips her makeup bag into it, opens the car door and steps out onto the parking lot.

She reveals a five foot, six, beautifully dressed woman in a white silk blouse, perfectly fitted size six designer jeans and six-inch red bottom heals. She takes on a super model officer-like stance as if she has been commissioned as a spy for a secret mission by James Bond himself.

Sandy, a pretty brown-skinned woman with mild features and a weave of long jet black waves, follows suit. As she steps out of the car and takes up her stance, she reveals a semi 70's outfit. She is wearing a colorful halter top and a black leather mini skirt to accent her well-shaped legs.

The two begin the journey through the parking lot to the door without exchanging any words. They rapidly walk past the long line of 70's characters. As they approach the front of the line, Bethany reaches inside her Louis Vuitton handbag, instantly pulls out a crisp one-hundred-dollar bill, and in the same motion, slips it into the hand of the bouncer at the door. Without missing a step, Bethany with Sandy not far behind, walks past the roped-off stanchions as if both women have done this a million times before.

Inside the club, the music is playing loudly. There are colorful disco balls hanging throughout the club and flashing lights that strobe to the beat of the music. The club is already crowded with men and women of all ages. Some mingling at the crowded bar, others already breaking a sweat on the high energy, spacious dance floor. The Commodores, "She's a Brick House" is booming over the loud sound system as Bethany and Sandy make their way to the crowded bar.

As they reach the bar, the song comes to an end and DJ "Big-Fro" takes the opportunity to speak to all the ladies. "I want to say hello to all the beautiful ladies in the house tonight. This is your night! I dedicate this next song to you, so get up off your seat, get out there on the dance floor and get your groove on! Don't be afraid to work up a sweat because in the next hour, all drinks are half off for all the ladies in the house! Hey, fellows, grab that girl standing next to you and do the bump! It's ladies' night!"

"It's Ladies' Night" by Cool and the Gang begins to play and the DJ starts singing along. Sandy yells out her drink order to her friend, "I'll have a double Long Island Iced Tea! You know this is my song! I'll be back before the drinks come." She dances off, doing the bump by herself as she makes her way to the dance floor. A guy dressed in an all-white, bell-bottomed, polyester three-piece suit and an exaggerated pompadour hairstyle joins her. He looks to be at least sixty years old, however, his youthful stamina is an even match for Sandy's thirty something energy.

Bethany gracefully glides into a newly emptied chair at the bar. On her left is a man sitting with his back towards her. She scopes him out, and judging by his wardrobe, she determines he's not her type. On the other side of her is a group of three men who have squeezed into a small space at the bar. One of the men is a bit too muscular for Bethany's taste. He is sitting in a chair while the other two are standing. The space is so tight that the rear of Bethany's chair is backed up against the rear of the guy's chair.

The three men are engaged in lively movement, immature horse playing and loud conversation among themselves. The muscular man's harsh movements cause his chair to knock up against hers. However, she tunes them out, assuming that the disturbance will come to a halt soon enough. Before she gets settled into her seat at the bar, she takes out another crisp one-hundred-dollar bill from her handbag and places it in the palm of her hand. She gets the attention of one of the many busy bartenders, flashes the incentive in the palm of her hand and proceeds to order a few drinks.

"I'll have a double Long Island Iced Tea and a Courvoisier with one ice cube. Keep your eye on me tonight and this is yours." She flashes the one-hundred-dollar bill again. The bartender gives Bethany a nod as he rushes off to make her drinks.

Bethany sits back in the bar seat, crosses her legs and leans one elbow on the bar.

She begins to settle into the seat that will be hers for the duration of the evening. Once again, she experiences bumping from the muscular man's chair. "Well, this is getting annoying," she thinks to herself as she gives her chair a harsh knock to make him aware of his disturbance. It proves to be of no use. She brushes it off once again and sinks back into her lounging position.

Bethany discreetly takes in the atmosphere of the club with piercing eyes. She scans the bar and then the dance floor area as if she's a skilled spy in a James Bond movie. The bartender comes back with her drinks, and Bethany reaches into her bag and comes up with slightly over the amount needed to pay for her drinks. Again, she flashes the one-hundred-dollar bill in the palm of her hand. She yells out, "Keep the change" as the bartender moves on to his next drink order.

She picks her drink up to her nose, inhales and begins to sip as she continues to scan the club. "My, my and my!" She thinks to herself. "Doesn't look like there's much to choose from tonight. Yep, some slim Pickens." She scans the crowd again, letting her eyes fall on one man and then another. "Too young, too old... too... I don't know, just too."

Suddenly, her eyes fall on a handsome man who is clean shaven, well-groomed and handsomely dressed in jeans and a tailored button down shirt. "Oh, who is this?" He starts walking in her direction and she perks up, but she tries not to let her interest in him be too obvious. She continues to have a dialogue with herself, "He looks like he smells good."

As he draws nearer to her, Bethany suddenly recognizes him. "Oops, did that!" she thinks to herself as she tries to shrink in her chair. They lock eyes, but he keeps going, pretending to not recognize her, and with a sigh of relief, she resumes her search. "Well, the evening is still young," she thinks to herself as she finishes the last sip of her Courvoisier. As she turns around, her eyes meet with her bartender, who begins to make his way toward her.

Before Bethany can open her mouth, a voice from the chair next to her yells to the bartender over the loud music. "I'll get that drink for the lady and I'll have a Sex on the Beach." The bartender waits for Bethany's approval. She quickly glances at the man from head to toe before nodding to the bartender to bring the drinks. The man seated next to her is now facing her. He is dressed in a wide brimmed black hat, a flashy red suit and matching red platform shoes. He flashes a gold-toothed smile.

"Now, this is going to be interesting," she thinks to herself. He speaks in a voice that is just as flashy as his wardrobe. "So, my bad; where are my manners? My name is Kalvin; that's with a K. Kalvin, with a K. And you are?" He reaches out his hand, expecting Bethany to comply with a handshake, but she doesn't, instead, she says, "Sally is my name. That's Sally with an S." Kalvin is not bright enough to figure out that Bethany is mocking him.

Meanwhile, the jesting coming from the men on the other side of Bethany is causing her to become more annoyed, because this time, the knocking up against her chair is more frequent. The bartender brings their drinks and Kalvin just about chokes when he hears the total for both drinks. He looks at Bethany from head to toe and then speaks, "Oh, you got a premium drink. I should have known ... a lady with your style and class."

Kalvin nervously reaches into his pocket and begins to count his one dollar bills, hoping he has enough money to cover the drinks. Suddenly, the chair next to Bethany jolts her chair so hard that she actually slips off her seat. She stumbles to the floor and quickly regains her composure without falling. The three men and Kalvin don't even notice that she's out of her chair until she goes and takes a brave stance in the midst of the annoying men.

Now that she is face-to-face with him, she notices that the man's muscles are even larger than what she'd imagined, but Bethany is undeterred. She stands with her hands on her hips, and without saying a word, draws back her foot high enough so that his two friends standing behind her can see her red bottom sole. As she swings her foot in the downward motion, the man with muscles bigger than life gets a good look at the pointed end of the same shoe as she violently makes contact with her target, giving him a swift kick in the shin.

Though he has a look of shock on his face, he appears to be unharmed by her assault. From Kalvin's perspective, however, the world has stopped. The music has faded, everyone is standing still, and he is paralyzed with fear. Bethany raises her voice above the loud music and yells at the man, "Stop all the knocking; will you?!" After a long moment of motionlessness from all parties, the man begins to slowly rise to his feet. By the time he is fully standing, he looks to be at least twelve feet tall as he towers over Kalvin's mere 5'3" frame. Bethany stands unmoved and fearless as if she is daring the giant to do something.

The giant turns his attention to Kalvin. Kalvin finally comes out of his frozen position, and as he finishes counting out his one dollar bills to the bartender, he looks at the giant, then to Bethany. He then turns back to the giant as if he is choosing which side to take. Bethany loses. "Um, man; she sorry," Kalvin says with the most apologetic face he can muster up. Then to Bethany he says, "Woman, tell the man you sorry!"

Not getting a response from Bethany, he says to the giant, "She sorry, man; but she not even with me... I thought she was a little off." He whispers to Bethany, "Tell the man you're a little off, girl!" The giant finally responds with a voice that is even more intimidating than his size. "Little man, I think we need to take this outside since you can't control your woman." He pounds his fist into his hand to frighten the coward even the more. Secretly, the giant and his friends are getting a kick out of seeing Kalvin squirm.

Meanwhile, as she watches, Bethany takes up her fresh drink from the bar, anticipating what's going to happen next. Kalvin continues to try to talk his way out of a beat down. "Man, I don't want any trouble; here, let me buy you a drink." He artfully snatches Bethany's drink out of her hand and shoves it into the giant's hand. Kalvin then snatches his drink off the bar and gets lost on the dance floor, mumbling complaints against Bethany. The giant and his friends chuckle at Kalvin's cowardly departure. Then the giant gives Bethany a nod of approval and raises his drink to her as if he were toasting her bravery.

As Bethany takes her seat, she beckons the bartender. He comes immediately and she orders a drink for herself, and as she glances at her watch, she orders another drink for Sandy. This time, however, she orders the Long Island Iced Tea with a triple shot. Just as she is finishing the order, Sandy, who is sweating and almost out of breath, shows up.

"Girl, where is my drink? I'm sweating up in here. A woman needs her drink." Bethany points to the now watered down drink as Sandy takes it up in her hand and drinks it down as if it were water. She finishes most of the drink and makes her usual complaint: "Chaney's needs to stop serving these watered-down drinks."

Bethany immediately snaps back, "No, my friend. You need to stop letting your drinks sit around on the bar for an hour." This is a discussion they share every time they go to the club, because every week,

Sandy and Bethany go through the same routine. Bethany sits at the bar ordering drinks for the night, while Sandy stays out on the dance floor much too long after having ordered her drink. "Well, okay then. Order me another Long Island Iced Tea," and then they both say in unison, "...only this time, make it a triple." They both chuckle at their silliness.

Suddenly, Bethany is pulled out of the moment with her friend as she locks eyes with someone in the distance. Sandy notices and looks in the direction that Bethany is looking and sees him too. With this, Sandy changes the joyful mood of the conversation to that of an instructional one, "Meet me back at the east bar at one a.m., otherwise, I'll know that you scored a date and I'll just get a ride home with Lynn tonight. I've already put her on notice. She knows to not leave without checking with me first. Have fun; be careful, and honey, he's kinda fine."

She then gives Bethany a thumbs up as she swallows down the remainder of her drink, slams the empty glass on the bar and then, grabs the fresh drink as the bartender delivers them to the women.

She's then swept off to the dance floor by the perfect timing of the man in the white suit and exaggerated pompadour hairstyle.

Bethany pays the bartender in the same manner as before, but this time, she hands over the one-hundred-dollar tip and shoots him a flirtatious wink. She settles back on her barstool, picks up her fresh Courvoisier and begins to sip her drink with class. She resumes locking eyes with the man who is now standing in front of her.

"Is this seat taken?" His voice is as smooth as butter. The giant and the three men have abandoned their headquarters for the evening, so Bethany nods as if to give him permission to take the seat next to her, while their eyes are still locked on one another. He takes a seat, while keeping his eyes fixed on the mysterious woman sitting in front of him. "You have some kind of audacity... I saw what you just did; pretty impressive. That took some heart! You know, I could get used to you... George is my name. Whom do I have the pleasure?"

Bethany quickly throws back the rest of her drink, sits her glass down and reaches out her hand to make contact with the gentleman's. "Bethany is my name and yes, I'll have a drink." George promptly calls the bartender over, orders drinks, turns to Bethany and begins to get to know his date for the evening.

At least an hour has gone by and the two are engaged in the same captivating stare at one another as they were at the beginning of their encounter. Judging by their body language, the conversation is a heated one. Meanwhile, dancing continues on the crowded dance floor and Sandy, who is now striking her Y.M.C.A poses to the Y.M.C.A song, locks eyes on the couple. After a few minutes, Bethany grabs her handbag as George rises to his feet, grabs Bethany by her hand, pulls her off the chair and begins to lead her through the crowd towards the exit. With that, they leave the club.

Sandy flags her friend, Lynn, down. "Girl, I am going to need that ride tonight. You don't mind; do you?" Lynn answers sarcastically, "Really?! Why am I not surprised? Sandy, this is nothing new. Every Thursday night, you flag me down to let me know you need a ride home. Nothing has changed. You ride here with Bethany and you hitch a ride home with me. Every Thursday night. I know the drill."

Sandy responds with a tinge of disgust in her voice, "Well, you know my girl, Bethany is on the prowl on Thursday nights. I guess she just can't help herself. That's my friend in all, but between me and you, I believe she has some issues, but we don't have to get into all that right now. Ooh, that's my song."

They both return to the dance floor as Kool and the Gang's, "Celebration" plays. The dance floor is lively. DJ Big-Fro begins to give another shout out to the ladies, warning them of last call for the bar. A Soul Train line is spontaneously formed and Sandy and the man in the white suit and pompadour hairstyle — her "Mr. Wrong" for the night — are seen cutting 70's dance moves as they shake their bodies down the soul train line.

Chapter Two

FRIDAY, ALL DAY!

It's early Friday morning and Bethany swiftly enters her kitchen, adjusting her beautifully tailored two-piece suit. She begins to go through her morning ritual of vitamin taking and coffee making. Her home phone rings and she opts to answer it by speaker so that she can continue to make her coffee.

"Hello." She pauses from her activity as she waits to see who is on the other end. A deep masculine voice comes out of the speaker. "Morning beautiful. I wanted to catch you before you started your busy day. Hey, charge your phone. I have been trying to call you since last night. I've called you a few times, but it kept going to voice mail."

Ignoring his instructions, Bethany responds, "Good morning, Winston; what's up?" Winston proceeds,

"Oh, I just wanted to confirm this evening's plans with you." There is an awkward silence for a moment because Bethany does not have a clue to what he is talking about. "Hello? You there?" Winston sounds like he's on his car's Bluetooth. "I'm here..." Bethany still does not have a clue.

Winston continues, "Soooo, I'll pick you up at your house at say around five-thirtyish or so? With that, he switches the tone in his voice for a moment. "Please be ready, Bethany. I don't want to be late. Oh, and can you check to see if I left the invitation there? It could be there on the dining table or the kitchen counter area..." Bethany, still puzzled, starts to move towards the dining table, but then notices the invitation on the counter. She picks it up and breathes a sigh of relief. She opens it quickly and begins to read it aloud. "The Mayor's Ball... yes... it's here."

Meanwhile, George, her pickup date from last night, enters from the bedroom area. He's adjusting his clothes as he begins to help himself to a cup of coffee. When Bethany sees him entering the kitchen, she quickly picks up the phone's receiver to discharge from the speaker. She casually finishes up her conversation with Winston, silently gesturing to George that she'll be finished in a moment. "Yes, 5:30 it is. Okay. See you then... uh huh... uh huh... yes, okay. Talk later. Alright. Have a good day."

George quickly swallows his first sip of coffee. "Who was that this early in the morning? Girl, you a go-getter, handling your business first thing in the morning." Ignoring his inquisition and comments, Bethany responds with a bit of coldness in her voice, "Did you find everything that you needed? Oh, there's an extra toothbrush in the lower cabinet in the bathroom."

George moves in close to Bethany, attempting to recreate the chemistry they shared the previous night, "Oh, that's okay. I used yours." A brief look of disgust flashes across Bethany's face as she dodges his advances. George continues, "So, when are we going to do this again? Like I told you last night, I can get used to you." He lunges for her again as Amber, Bethany's teenage daughter, enters the kitchen area from her bedroom.

Amber looks a lot like her mother, but younger. She is obviously disturbed by what she encounters this early in the morning. However, she is not surprised to see a strange man in the house and it is evident in the tone of her greeting. "Good morning... so mom, I need..."

Bethany cuts her off by turning to George as if on a mission to hasten his departure. Bethany speaks in a low voice, but not a whisper, "So, maybe we can do this again. I have your number; right?" George eagerly responds in a tone matching hers, "Yeah; yeah, right! I left my card somewhere you can find it; you know, just in case you haven't locked my phone number into your phone yet." He gives her a corny, exaggerated wink.

Bethany is turned off by his corny wink and shows it. He tries to put his manhood back on as she walks him to the door and positions him on the other side of the threshold. Bethany whispers in a condescending tone, "Alright then. I had a nice time last night. See you later... or soon... or sometime; good bye. She closes the door and walks back into the kitchen where Amber is making herself a bowl of cereal.

"So, mom ... tonight, I have a youth meeting at my church and this is the last day to pay the registration fee for the upcoming youth conference. You keep forgetting to write the check... can you do it now?" Bethany cuts her daughter off as she looks at her watch. "Not now. I'm late, Amber. I have to get to my office. Do you have gas in your car? Oh, and please wake your brother up in a few minutes. You know if he doesn't have enough time to get ready for school, he forgets something ... then he's calling me in the middle of the day, asking me to stop what I'm doing to bring him what he left at home."

Bethany begins to busy herself by gathering her keys and belongings. "I'll write a check and put it on the counter when I get home this afternoon. I probably won't be here when you get home this evening from school. I have the Mayor's ball with Winston... which I completely forgot about..." Amber mumbles something under her breath and shrugs her shoulders. Bethany pretends she doesn't notice her daughter's behavior. "I have to stop by the cleaners to get that black dress. I probably should just take an extra-long lunch and shop for a new dress. Yes, that's what I'll do." Bethany leaves the house and shuts the door.

There is a moment of silence as Amber continues to eat her cereal. Suddenly, Bethany pokes her head back in the door and reaches her hand in with a hundred-dollar bill. "Amber, how much is the registration fee? Will this hundred cover it? This should cover it...come get this... Oh, I'll just toss it right here; come get it... have a good day."

With that, the door closes again. Amber, a pretty mature sixteen-year-old, takes her time and finishes her bowl of cereal, walks to the sink, rinses the bowl and then goes to pick the money up by the door. With the same pace, she starts towards her bedroom, making a brief stop at her brother's bedroom door. She gives the door a soft knock, and with a stern womanly voice, she speaks to her brother, "David, Jr.! It's time to get up." She waits for a moment and then puts her ear to the door.

When she hears movement, she continues to her own bedroom.

Hours later, the house is quiet. The evening's setting sun has cast a brilliant orange light through Bethany's delicate ivory colored lace draperies. Underneath the draperies is a four-paneled picture window. The picture window could be the focal point of the immaculate living room if it weren't for the modernized whitewashed brick fireplace that seems to cover an entire wall. It's a masterpiece in itself.

Then, of course, there is the beautiful white shabby chic sectional couch, made of a high-quality linen. This and the twelve-seating dining room table made of dark oak seems to give the living room space a sense of family and homeyness. The dining room table is set with elegant china and accented with gold trimmed glass and flatware.

The kitchen, which sits off the living room, is functional and reflects Bethany's sensibility. It's loaded with all the high-end amenities that one could ask for. The ivory-colored marble countertops are filled with all the latest gadgets, and the glass breakfast table is surrounded by white leather chairs; it makes for a cozy place to sit, especially for a casual family meal.

The doorbell rings and its elegant chimes seem to bring life to the house ... a house that, in the moment before, seemed empty, peaceful and asleep. Bethany emerges from her bedroom, beautifully dressed and polished in her new red dress. Her dark, curly tresses have been gracefully pulled into an up-do hairstyle, showing off Bethany's beautiful bone structure. She opens the door expecting to greet Winston, but is instead greeted by George.

With flowers in his hand, George stares at Bethany in approval. "Wow, you look good. That dress is saying something... looks like I'm just in time." Bethany cuts him off. "George, what are you doing here?" As he invites himself in, he speaks in a tone that would suggest that he and Bethany are long time mates. "Oh, baby, I was just in the neighborhood and I thought I would just swing by.

Where you going? Can I go? It just so happens that I have a suit in my car."

There is an awkward moment and then George speaks again, remembering the flowers in his hand this time. "Here, I brought these roses for a rose… like you." Bethany is not impressed. She is at a loss for words and makes no effort to receive the flowers he's offered her. Ignoring her rude gesture, he continues to make attempts to get his way. "I thought we could have a little repeat of last night. I told you I could get used to you." He tries to move in close to her for an intimate moment, but she pushes him away. "George, I have plans tonight. Besides, I don't appreciate you just dropping in at my house unannounced. Please call the next time."

Bethany begins to show George to the door, but he objects, "Alright; that's fair. I should have called first; my bad. But, can you just take a moment with me?" His tone thickens and begins to sound more aggressive. "I came all this way; don't you want your flowers?" Bethany is lightly pushing him towards the door. The tone in his voice becomes even more hostile and the moment becomes a little tense as he turns and moves towards Bethany.

By now, he's standing directly in front of Bethany and begins to glare at her with confrontational eyes. "How are you just going to rush me out? This is a little rude; don't you think? Not even grateful for your flowers!" He stares her down with coldness in his eyes, but Bethany refuses to be intimidated in her own home. She takes a moment and then, with a seriously stern voice, takes a stand against his nonsense.

"You know what?! Lose my number and forget where I live! Now go!" She points to the door with a look on her face that makes it clear that she won't be changing her mind. They each stare at one another as if they are cowboys in a western gun draw, each waiting for the other to make even the slightest move. After another tense moment, George finally gives in and decides to leave, but not before giving Bethany a tongue lashing.

"Alright. I'm going and I will lose your number. I will even forget where you live... because you aren't all that... you're just a waste of my time anyway... I got other play things..." Bethany continues to escort George to the door, and as he steps over the threshold, she speaks to him in the same stern tone, "Good for you; go play then..." She slams the door in his face, braces her body against the shut door, puts her hand over her racing heart and finishes saying what she wasn't brave enough to say to his face: "...little boy!"

There is a long moment of silence wherein Bethany tries to calm herself down and regain her composure. The doorbell chimes ring out again and Bethany smooths out her dress, pats her hair, takes a deep breath and then exhales. A few seconds later, a composed Bethany answers the door. The opened door reveals a handsome brown-skinned man who stands at least 6'4." His well-groomed hair and perfectly lined beard is peppered with a slight hint of gray. His abs are firm, revealing a slight protrusion, but other than that, he is a fit, athletically built man. His graying hair, slightly plump belly, along with his good looks, enhances his wise and mature demeanor.

"Hey beautiful." Winston greets her with a kiss on the cheek. "Who was that just leaving?" Bethany answers back with a whimsical attitude, "An old friend... so, would you like a drink before we leave?" Winston looks at his watch before responding, "No, thank you, my lady; we better head out." Bethany grabs her matching silk pashmina and her Chanel clutch. She then reaches for the invitation sitting on the counter and hands it to Winston.

"Alright, we are off to our evening, my gentleman." She does sort of a curtsy as if she's at an eighteenth-century ball, responding to his invitation to dance. Winston responds with an obligated bow. "It's an honor, my lady," he responds. They both stroll to the door, and with Bethany's arm in his, Winston leads the way. In his true gentlemanly nature, he opens the door, sees that she's first out, and then closes it behind them.

Moments later, Amber, along with her friend, Wendy, burst through the door. Their youthful energy and lively conversation brings a different type of vibe to the atmosphere of the home.

Amber's friend, Wendy, has a nice contrast in appearance compared to Amber. Amber is petite in size and stature, has long curly hair and a fair complexion.

Wendy, on the other hand, is a little on the chubby side, stands at least six inches above her best friend and wears her hair in long braid extensions. Wendy's jovial personality can sometimes convey that she's not-so-bright, however, Wendy is at the top of her class academically; that is, when she applies herself. Amber's responsible attitude and maturity helps Wendy to stay focused on achieving her goals.

The two young women have just encountered Winston and Bethany on their way in, and as usual, Wendy is enamored with Bethany's beauty and class. "Your mother is so pretty. She always be dressed to the t ... man, I love that dress she got on... I wonder if it would fit me..." Amber gives her friend a side-eyed glare. "Wendy, where you going to wear that dress to?" Wendy confidently responds, "To prom." Amber gives her friend another side-eyed glare. Wendy rethinks her

answer and offers an alternative. "Well, next year...
I'm just saying." With that, she changes the subject.
"Mr. Winston is fine... ain't he? To be an older man,
you know he fine..." Amber breaks her friend's line
of thinking. "I don't know, Wendy. I don't be paying
attention like that."

In walks David Jr., Amber's younger brother. He is a
handsome fifteen-year-old who, by the manner of
his disheveled wardrobe, neglected head of curls
and air of mystery, makes him appear to be a
troubled kid. He heads directly towards his
bedroom without saying a word or making eye
contact with either of the girls. Amber follows him
with her eyes as he crosses to his room. Obviously
annoyed at the appearance of her brother or
perhaps by her friend's comment about Winston,
she snaps at Wendy.

"Can we change the subject, Wendy?" Wendy is all
too eager to change the subject. "Okay. Yeah,
because I have something else to talk about ... well
SOMEONE else to talk about..." She takes a moment,
bats her eyes and then covers her heart with both
hands. She takes another dramatic moment and

afterwards, blurts out her secret to her best friend. "Joey Carter! Girl, I caught him looking at me today. You know, I think I just might be getting me a boyfriend soon."

Wendy pulls out her cell phone and begins to make her way to Joey Carter's Facebook page. "He answered my friend request on Facebook today." She clicks on his photos. "Now, you know this boy is fine. Look at that body. A football player indeed" Wendy begins to enlarge his photo. Once his photo is enlarged, she scrolls down past his nose until nothing but his lips can be seen on her phone. She then proceeds to kiss her phone as Amber looks on with amazement. Wendy continues to peruse his Facebook page, but Amber is obviously distracted. She excuses herself, takes the few steps down the hallway to David's room and quickly disappears inside.

Wendy gets to her feet and begins to find places in the immaculate home to take selfies of herself. For the next few moments, Wendy takes several selfies in different poses. First, she stands in front of the floor modeled double-sided mirror so that her backside is reflected in the picture. Then, she takes several of herself sitting at the elegant dining table so that the chinaware makes her look like she's on the date of her life. Next, she takes another picture standing in front of the white-washed fireplace.

As she's snapping one selfie after another, she's also having an imaginary conversation with Joey Carter out loud with herself. The sudden ring of Amber's cell phone startles her for a moment and as she returns to answer it, she stops taking pictures and instead begins to post her selfies to his wall. Her imaginary conversation with her new crush is cut short when Amber returns. Amber grabs her ringing cell phone from her school bag, gets a glimpse of the caller ID and immediately her demeanor changes.

In her happiest voice, she proceeds to greet the person on the other end, "Hello Mama Nettie. What you doing? Your car? What's wrong with it?" She listens intently to her Grandmother's explanation, then cuts her off to settle the problem. "Mama Nettie, Mama Nettie; listen… don't worry about your car right now. Why don't I just come pick you up and bring you to youth Bible study with us? We can just leave here a little bit earlier. Yes, you know I don't miss Bible study. Pack a bag and just stay over until Sunday night, and after Uncle Ben's birthday dinner, I'll bring you home. We can get Mr. Thompson to check out your car over the weekend. Yes, ma'am. There; settled!"

After that, she closes the deal like an expert salesperson, "Call Mr. Thompson now and tell him to come tow it!" She beams with pride as she listens to her grandmother's comments and then answers, "From you, Nettie. I get my smarts from you. Okay, we will see you in a little bit. Goodbye." Meanwhile, Wendy has stopped what she was doing to listen to the last few words of her friend's conversation. With a worried look on her face, she makes her inquiry, "You are dropping me off at home before YOU go to Bible study ... right?!"

Amber makes a smug reply, "Nope. You need it... your flesh is a mess... I saw you taking all those selfies... what you do with those pictures, Wendy?!" Wendy is tight-lipped and shows relief when the doorbell interrupts their conversation. Amber walks towards the door as she continues to admonish her friend, determined to not let her off the hook. "You don't have to say nothing, because I know what you did... you posted them on Joey's wall... Girl, you're coming to Bible study; you need Jesus." Amber opens the door and in walks the Attaway twins.

The Attaway twins, Cherlene and Berlene, are Bethany's well-meaning, nosy neighbors. The twins live on the opposite side of the street, towards the end of the block. Their house is situated in such a way that they can almost effortlessly see the comings and goings of the Clearwater household. These fifty something old maids are childless and have never been married. Fraternal twins, they look nothing alike.

Cherlene stands a towering 5'9", has a robust full-figured body frame and a lovely dark brown skin tone, while Berlene is a much shorter, average built woman who is at least five shades lighter than her twin. The most common attributes these sisters share are their almost identical hand and body jesters and how they tend to finish each other's sentences, often saying the same thing at the same time.

Berlene steps into the house first and greets Amber and Wendy. "Hi there, Amber. Wendy, how you doing? How's your mother? Let her know we want our hair done next week." She quickly retracts her request, "That's okay. I'll just call her... I know how y'all kids are ... say you'll do something, but then, forget to do it... Lord knows we need our hair done."

Cherlene breaks in on her sister's train of thought, "Amber, we come to get the food your mother wants us to cook for Sunday. She said it would be in the freezer and some in the fridge. Y'all going to have a party for your Uncle Ben now; right? That's going to make him feel really good."

Amber beams with joy at the thought of seeing her one and only uncle soon. "I know, Ms. Cherlene. I haven't seen Uncle Ben since..." Suddenly, her mood shifts as if she's remembering something she has no desire to remember. "Well, for a few months." She closes the conversation abruptly. "Can you help yourselves with that stuff? We're off to Bible study right now."

Cherlene replies, "Sure honey; go on. Tell Pastor to pray for us." Suddenly, she retracts her request as quickly as her sister did earlier. "Never mind. I'll just give him a call... I know how y'all kids are ... say you'll do something, but then, forget to do it... Lord knows we need some prayer." Amber and Wendy side-eye one another and chuckle at the identical thought pattern of the two sisters.

Amber excuses herself, crosses to David's bedroom door and slips behind it. Wendy has pulled her over-sized makeup bag out and started "beating" her face. She puts on too much makeup, all the while, making facial expressions as if she is a super model in front of a camera throughout the process. The Attaway Twins watch this process with amazement and Cherlene expresses what both are thinking under her breath: "It's only Bible study..."

When Amber returns, she has her Bible in hand and an obviously agitated David. She gathers her purse and keys, and without looking up, gives her friend a command. "Come on, Wendy!" Wendy does not respond, so Amber looks in Wendy's direction and is startled by what she sees. Wendy is putting the finishing touches on her Vegas show girl themed makeup. "Really?!" screams Amber in dismay. Wendy gives her friend a smug, proud look as if to convey that she likes her makeup and is not taking it off.

She gathers her things and heads to the door with Amber and David as Berlene tries to engage David in conversation. "Well, hello there, David Jr. How you doing? Looking just like your daddy... Cherlene, isn't he looking more and more like his daddy?" Truthfully, David is the portrait of his father, but he's not having anything to do with this topic, so he responds with mumbling and inaudible words.

Cherlene chimes in with an exaggerated smile on her face as her eagle eyes fix on David. "Yes indeed ... just like his daddy." Amber decides to rescue her brother from the twins' harassment by hastening their departure, "Okay. We will see you later. You can see yourselves out; right? Just remember to lock the bottom lock. Thanks."

They leave and no sooner than the kids can get out of the door, the twins begin to discuss their thoughts on David Jr. and the Clearwater family. Berlene begins by stating the obvious.

"Cherlene, something is not right with that boy!" "I know Berlene... something not right and whatever it is didn't just happen overnight. That boy been troubled for a long time, but that thing that happened a few months ago, that really sent him over the edge, I think." Cherlene agrees with her sister. "I know. And here they go again, another family gathering... shaking my holy head."

"Yes. It may just very well be that some families are not meant to dwell together in harmony... Yup! They just might be gluttons for punishment."

"You may have a point, Berlene. Those poor kids... they really missed out on having a good father. He was a good man. Too bad he died... much too young... I feel sorry for them."

There are a few moments of silence as they continue to gather up the food, packing it up carefully in the Whole Food shopping bags they've found in the pantry. Berlene is working from the freezer and her sister from the refrigerator. Both are working systematically as if they are professional baggers at the local grocery store. They work like this for a few more moments with Berlene spending a few moments choosing the right spices from the elaborate spice rack in the middle of the countertop and Cherlene concentrating on a few corning ware dishes from the overhead cupboard.

Berlene briefly walks back into the walk-in food pantry and brings out a large cardboard box before she breaks the silence. "I feel sorry for Savannah. Now, you know she have her faults, but how she puts up with her sister... Bethany needs to stop with all her evil ways!"

They both begin to load up the bags and dishes into the box and Charlene chimes in once again with a little edge in her voice — almost as if she's making a bet with her sister.

"Berlene, I wonder if Savannah is going to show up for round two?"

"Round two? Cherlene, don't' you mean round three, four ..."

Berlene rolls her beady eyes to the back of her head as if she's trying to recall each instance in a matter of a few seconds. Then she shares her calculations. "Let's say... fifty-eleven times? They have been at each other's throats for years... and poor Mama Netty."

"Berlene, Savannah going to show up because Mama Netty will make sure of it." After that, she sticks out her hand to start a bet with her sister. "It's a bet. I get twenty dollars if Savannah shows up."

Berlene locks hands with her to seal the deal. "Deal then; I get twenty dollars if she doesn't." They shake on it.

Cherlene continues to showboat the strength of her case by pointing out something they both know. "Berlene, now that's one woman who can keep Bethany at bay, Mama Netty... yes, if it weren't for her, I don't know what would've become of those children... I think Bethany just going through the motions in life... she always gone..."

Berlene cuts her off and says, "Cherlene, you mean that she's always gone... with a man. Did you see she had another one the other night?" She thinks for a moment, and then says, "I have never seen him before…"

Her sister offers juicier gossip to the conversation. "Did you see he was back over this evening and actually left as Winston was arriving? How that man doesn't see he is not the only one is beyond me… and he is a nice man; he seems like he got it all together."

They each grab an end of the now fully loaded box with both their hands and begin to make their way to the door as Berlene closes their conversation about the Clearwaters for the evening. "Let's just make this food extra special…cause we going to need some good food to go along with this good entertainment that's getting ready to happen on Sunday." She balances the box in one hand for one moment as she flicks the bottom lock on the door. They maneuver the heavy box out the door with perfect teamwork as Cherlene grabs the door with her foot and pulls it shut.

It's now just before midnight and the house would be pitch black if it weren't for the full moon that shines through the four-paneled glass picture window. The decorative shadow from the lace window curtain gives the room an eerie mood and a restless David Jr. is seated quietly on the sofa in the dark; he is in deep thought. He brings to the room his own sadness. Even with the wrestling of the keys and faint voices that can be heard on the other side of the door, there is no movement from the teenager.

Moments later, a flirty Bethany and Winston break the gloomy mood with their romantic one. "So, you didn't answer my question. Would you like a nightcap?" Before Winston has an opportunity to answer, Bethany turns on the light and David jumps to his feet and startles the couple. "David Jr.!" Bethany turns her attention from Winston to her son. "How many times have I told you not to do that? Turn on the lights when you sit out here; only crazy men sit in the dark. Go to bed anyway; it's after midnight... what are you still doing up anyway?!... sitting in the dark!"

David quietly and mechanically goes to his bedroom. Bethany continues with her rant, but not necessarily to Winston. "Honestly, I don't know what's gotten into him. I'm about fed up with it though!" "Bethany," Winston interrupts. He has a look on his face as if he is trying to choose his words carefully. He motions her over to the couch where he is about to take a seat. "Do you think David might be troubled emotionally?" Bethany takes a seat next to Winston as he carefully continues. "I've watched him... it seems that he's becoming more and more withdrawn and his personality has changed dramatically over these past..."

Bethany abruptly cuts him off. "Please Winston; save it. There is nothing wrong with David. He's just seeking extra attention. He's just trying me, but I'm not buying into his manipulative tactics." Winston further tries to reason with her, "No Bethany; this looks a little deeper than just teenaged growing pains... I think you should take him to a professional..." Bethany cuts Winston off again, but this time, she closes the door on the conversation. "Winston, I know my son... Now, there's nothing more to discuss about David Jr." Winston intentionally remains silent for a few seconds, hoping to change the mood. "Alright Bethany," he says. "My apologies…"

There is another moment of silence, but this time, it's an awkward one. Winston speaks first. "Well, did you enjoy yourself this evening?" Bethany quickly gives an answer, giggling as if she hadn't been offended a few seconds earlier. "Yes, until you left me alone with Councilwoman Delaney. Winston, you know that was not right. That woman just went on and on and on. You know, I might just vote for her in the next election though because… at least she's persistent…"

They share a laugh and then, Winston takes Bethany's hand in his for a serious moment. "Bethany." He takes a deep breath and straightforwardly continues. "You know I love you." Bethany casually responds to him as if she's responding to a good friend, "I love you too, Winston…" Winston continues, "No, Bethany… I love you…" Then, he finds the right words to express what he's trying to say, "I'm in love with you. I think you know this." He deliberately makes contact with her eyes and says, "I need to talk with you about our relationship."

Bethany finds it difficult to hide her discomfort as she responds to him. "Okay... but Winston." Winston cuts her off to reassure her of his intentions. "I have always honored our "understanding," but the truth is Bethany, since I've met you, you've been the only woman in my life. I have not felt the need or the desire for any other... you are an amazing woman." Bethany withdraws her hands out of his as she objects to the direction that the conversation is heading in. "Winston... now, you know..."

Winston gently takes her hands again, gives her a resolved smile and continues. "Just hear me out, Bethany, and then, I promise you I'll hold my peace regardless of what you say. I just need to have this conversation... I think it's time." Bethany's mind begins to race as fast as her heart is beating, but all she can get to come out of her mouth is one word. "Okay?" she utters with uncertainty. But nevertheless, her inside voice was screaming, "No, it's not okay ... not okay at all! Winston, we have an unspoken understanding... please don't cross that line because if you do, I will have to cut you off and I really don't want to. After all, I like you; I like us just the way we are. No changes! Change is not good!"

Winston continues with a sincere and a kind of sappy tone, "I've watched you come through a lot, Bethany. Single mom, starting your own business... As your lawyer, I could not have been more proud watching you take hold of courage and using it to your advantage. You have accomplished in your business everything you started out to do and then some. When it comes to you in business, I'm your biggest fan..."

Bethany nervously musters up enough strength to respond, "Why thank you, Winston... why do I feel like there is a but coming..." Winston knows this may be his one and only chance to say what he needs to say, so he cuts her off, not willing for her to break his flow and courage. "You're a strong woman who's witty, charming and quite frankly, a lot of fun to spend time with. I enjoy you..."

Bethany is absolutely beside herself as one of her most favorite traits in the man she thinks of as her "safe zone" begins to surface; his eloquent vulnerability. He lays his heart on the table without losing his dignity. He continues, "I hope I don't sound corny, but it's the truth about you, Bethany. Sometimes, I get the feeling you really don't know just how much of a joy you are and how precious you are... not a lot of people have what you have. I don't know how to explain it...but you have it."

Bethany is a bit humored as she breaks his flow again. Her interjection confirms what Winston is saying; she doesn't understand that she has 'it.' "Winston ...," Bethany says with a bit of a nervous giggle. "... what is "it?" Winston continues, "All I know, Bethany, is that I get you... I get it ... I've watched you when you didn't know I was paying attention. At your most vulnerable times, I've watched you... with your family, your sister, Savannah, ... your children...and then, there is me. I get to see the secret side to you that no one else gets to see... what I figured out is that you are a tenacious business woman who has pushed herself hard for her family... and not necessarily for a successful business."

Bethany tries to interject again, but Winston puts his two fingers over her lips to prevent her from speaking. He continues with, "I've seen glimpses of that hidden treasure, that thing that is inexplicable, but everyone wants. Deep down you yearn to be appreciated and you desire to have again what you once had in your family. You desire to be loved and to have genuine love working in your life and relationships again... it's what you've always desired... Your tenacity helped you obtain that once... unfortunately, you lost your husband and somehow, you thought you had to lose the right to be loved... or to have it in your relationships..."

Inwardly, Bethany tells herself to stop this man from exposing her secrets and her heart is admonishing her for letting herself become so careless with her secrets. What comes out of her mouth is an attempt to cover up this truth. She casually says, "Look Winston, I can appreciate you thinking you have me all figured out, but I..." He cuts her off yet again, as he senses her panic over having been found and begins to reassure her that she is still safe to be herself with him, that indeed, nothing has changed.

"Don't worry, Bethany," he says with a reassuring voice. "I'm not proposing marriage... I just want you to know that I see you. I can't say that I have you all figured out, but I am paying attention. To some, it would look like you live in a house of misery ... but that's just conflict in you that needs to be resolved. I want you to know I'm here and I care..."

Bethany breathes a sigh of relief and asks, "Winston, what are you saying...? I don't understand what you want from me..." Winston finds the perfect words to close his much-needed conversation with Bethany, "For now, I'm just proposing that you take notice..." After those words, he looks directly into her eyes and says, "Perhaps, one day I can help you turn your house of misery into a house of joy and song again..."

Bethany is finally feeling the relief she has been seeking throughout this uncomfortable conversation and is all too obliged to change the mood. "Well, Mr. Winston, I like things just the way they are... and I'm paying attention too..." He responds just as lighthearted, "You're paying attention?" Bethany cuts him short to take advantage of the moment and makes a request on a long-standing proposition, "Umm hmmm, and to prove it, why don't you stay the night so I can show you just how much..."

At this moment, Bethany is wondering why she is allowing these words to come out of her mouth since she knows Winston's strong objection to this proposition. The understanding comes to her like a fleeting moment. Subconsciously, she needs to test him to make sure everything is still the same between them." Winston's answer brings the relief she is hoping for. "Uhhh, Bethany... now, you know how I feel about that... situation..." Bethany decides to play it all the way out just to make sure he's still solid.

"What? Come on, Winston; we are grown.... when are you going to get over that hang-up? It's Friday anyway..." Winston is not budging from his principles. He interrupts, "And tomorrow is

Saturday. Your children will be here, and what happens when they see a man so early in the morning?! Bethany, come on... we've already settled this discussion. You know where I stand, pretty lady. As much as I'd like to..." Her heart leaps for joy as she lets up on the pressure.

"Okay, okay, okay... Winston... I know you are not budging...Let's just change the subject. So, are you going to make it to our dinner for Uncle Benjamin Sunday? You know we would love to have you." She lets out an awkward giggle, and then finishes her thought with, "to keep the peace." Getting the joke, Winston chuckles at the image of their family dinner. He then answers with, "Regrettably, Bethany, I can't make it on Sunday. I have to meet a client up north. I sure would like to see Uncle Benjamin though. How long is he in town for?"

Bethany giggles again as she reassures him that he will see Uncle Benjamin. "Oh, I'm sure he'll be here for a while as he always wears out his welcome when he comes for a visit... I mean that in a good way... really..." Winston rises to his feet as he prepares to say good night to the love of his life.

"Bethany, what am I going to do with you?" Bethany returns to the same flirty tone she had at the beginning of this conversation, "What? You know you love me."

As Winston takes her by the hand and strolls to the door, he gazes into her eyes once again and affirms her words. "That, I do... That, I do Bethany..." He gently caresses her face in each of his hands and says, "Well, good night, Bethany. As always, I've had a marvelous time." He gently leans forward and kisses her forehead before bidding her good night once again. "Well, good night, lovely lady." With that, Winston opens the door and leaves. Bethany softly shuts the door behind him and stays by the door, enjoying the lingering scent of his cologne.

Chapter Three

WORK OUT OR WORK OVER

Bethany enters the kitchen area for her morning ritual of vitamin taking and coffee, which she brewed earlier. Dressed in her workout gear, she heads to the kitchen table to enjoy her cup of Joe and a little quiet time before going to the gym for her boot camp class. Suddenly, the sound of the doorbell's chimes interrupts her peace. She answers the door to see a bright-eyed, high energy Sandy Leach, also dressed in her workout gear.

"Sandy, you a little early this morning, I said seven o'clock, not six..." Sandy doesn't wait for an invite, but enters the house and proceeds to the coffee as she responds. "I know, girl... I was up a little earlier than usual this morning. Thought I would come over and have coffee with my friend before we head off to the gym." Bethany gives her friend a brief look of suspicion, which goes unnoticed by Sandy.

After they both settle at the table, Sandy starts a casual conversation. "So, what's going on? How was your week? Oh, how was that little rendezvousing with um; what was his name? Did it turn into a date?" Bethany looks at her friend as if she doesn't understand what her friend is referring to. Sandy continues to pry, "Bethany, you know what I'm talking about!" Sandy becomes quiet as she waits for her friend to respond. Bethany doesn't respond fast enough, so Sandy continues. "Did it turn into an overnight date?"

Sandy already knows the answer, nevertheless, she waits for a response because this is one of the games they both play to keep the pretense up in their friendship. Sandy pretends to care and Bethany pretends to be too naïve to know that Sandy is only pretending to care. After a well-timed moment, they both burst into laughter and Bethany proceeds to give a brief description. "Yes, it was one of those nights..." Sandy continues to inquire, "... Well? How was it?... How was he?... Is he a keeper?"

Bethany responds with just enough information to stop her nosy friend's inquiry. "Let's just say... he lost my phone number and house address… at my request…" Sandy responds with a tinge of pretentious disappointment in her voice. "That bad; huh? Such a waste then cause he was kinda fine… but Bethany, you might need to stay away from Chaney's on ladies' night… you're averaging a no hitter."

They both laugh as Sandy realizes yet again, that she's not going to get the gritty details of Bethany's intimate life. They are not the kind of friends who exchange secrets about lovers or have lunch dates, shopping trips or long telephone conversations discussing their goals and aspirations in life. However, Sandy never ceases to challenge Bethany so, as she always does, she brings up the man who she views as Bethany's 'home run'.

"How is Mr. Winston, with his fine self? Girl, why don't you just get serious with him? If you don't want him, I'll take him. He got it all together. A good job, drive a nice car, look good, dress good, smell good… manners… drama free…" Sandy falls into a private fantasy moment with Winston as Bethany looks on with amusement. As she comes out of the

moment, there is a bit of an awkward silence
between the two and Sandy adjusts her voice to a
quieter and more serious tone. "Um, Bethany, I
need your help this month... I'm a little short on my
mortgage. I entered this credit repair program, and
if I'm late on paying my mortgage, it will go against
my credit... and then it'll be just like starting over..."

Mama Netty, who is heading up the hall from the
bedroom area to the kitchen, has overheard Sandy's
request and she quickly backs up a few steps out of
eye shot to eavesdrop on her daughter-in-law's
conversation. She wonders to herself when things
are going to change between these two women,
who have absolutely nothing in common with one
another.

Indeed, not much has changed about their
relationship since the night they met. Bethany just
happened to be sitting at the bar when Sandy came
up short trying to pay for her drink at Chaney's.
Sandy was in the process of using the "I changed my
handbag and forgot my wallet" excuse when
Bethany flashed the one-hundred-dollar bill in the
palm of her hand to the bartender.

For the rest of the evening, Sandy's bar tab was covered by Bethany's wealth. The two became acquainted through the small talk exchanged between them after Sandy would spend time dancing to her favorite seventies songs with a whole lot of "Mr. Wrongs." After that, she would come back to the bar to quench her thirst. So, their relationship has remained in much of the state that it began in — Sandy with her hand out and Bethany extending her generosity.

In fact, in the few years that they've known one another, Sandy has learned very little about Bethany. As far as she can figure, Bethany's wealth, handy cash, big house and high-end lifestyle does not come from the business Bethany owns, but from her deceased husband's life insurance policy. She has no idea that the woman she calls friend is a hard-working self-made millionaire, and it is no wonder.

After all, Sandy's perception is limited to the boundaries set forth by Bethany and they are: Thursday is ladies' night and Saturday is for workouts. Sandy has never been invited into the other side of Bethany's world, therefore, the thriving advertising firm Bethany has built from the ground up will never serve as a testament to the true essence of who she is in Sandy's eyes. But this is alright by Bethany because she lives by a strict code: never mix business with pleasure.

Bethany keeps her composure as she responds to her needy friend. "Well Sandy, how much do you need? How much do you have?" Sandy quickly responds, "Just two hundred..." Bethany looks to be pleasantly surprised by the amount needed, "Alright, I'll write you a check for two hundred...," but Sandy quickly corrects her friend. "No, I'm sorry. All I have is two hundred; I need to borrow one thousand..."

Bethany is flabbergasted for a moment, but not at all surprised at Sandy's request. Mama Netty is absolutely livid and is having a difficult time keeping her composure. For Mama Netty, it's not so much the money as it is the principle behind this whole pointless arrangement. Bethany continues, "Sandy, this puts you at about thirteen thousand ... or close to it that you'll owe me now...".

Upon hearing this bit of information, Mama Netty tries to contain her rage and fight the urge to go right over and shove Sandy right out of the front door and out of Bethany's life for good. But Bethany calmly changes the mood as she rises to get her checkbook out of her handbag and begins to write the check. "I think I better put you on a payment plan already," says Bethany as she fills out the check.

Sandy is about ten years younger than Bethany and is far inferior to Bethany both financially and intellectually. However, what Sandy lacks in financial earnings and intelligence, she makes up for in street smarts. She has a remarkable ability to recognize a good opportunity to prey on the weak and she lacks the integrity of heart that would prevent her from taking full advantage of that good thing. She has no problem asking for what she wants. But even her crafty and cunning ways are no match for Bethany's wisdom.

Truthfully, Bethany knows the check that she is about to write is not a loan, and she has no expectation of ever recovering any of the money she has given Sandy over the past few years. She considers it her "peace of mind" payoff, after all, both women have an understanding. When it comes to the low life, Sandy is her ride-or-die buddy in exchange for her money; this is an unwritten code both follow. When it comes to Bethany's life, Sandy knows she shouldn't ask any questions about who, what, where, when and how (in reference to Bethany's life). She also knows to not expect any emotional support or friendship beyond the club and workouts. These benefits are priceless in Bethany's mind.

Bethany adds her signature and hands the check to Sandy as Mama Netty makes her presence known. In the most exaggerated, loudest and most obvious way that she possibly can, she clears her throat. Sandy quickly tucks the check in her bosom as a startled Bethany makes her way to her mother-in-law. She greets her with a hug and a kiss. "Ma; what are you doing here?" asks Bethany. Mama Netty, locks eyes with Sandy (letting her know that she's on to her) and answers. "Good morning. I had Amber to come get me last night. How you doing, Sandy?" Sandy feels the coldness. "Oh, I'm good,

Mama Netty; thank you. And you?" Mama Netty doesn't respond. Instead, she heads into the kitchen, pours herself a cup of coffee and then begins to make breakfast for her grand-kids.

Bethany sits back at the table with Sandy to finish her coffee. "Sandy, we better finish up this fuel for this boot camp class. You know Boa will have us working... I hope we don't have to do any bear claws today." Sandy begins to examine her fingernails on cue. "I know," she says, "but bear claws have your backside looking good; this class be hard on my fingernails though. You mind if we stop off to Deborah's Nail Salon afterwards? You know, she's your friend and I can't get no good service or a discount unless you with me... uh, unless you're treating me today."

Mama Netty drops a pan in protest to Sandy's latest request. Bethany and Sandy both turn to investigate, but Mama Netty plays it off as if she's intentionally refusing to intervene in her daughter-in-law's business. Bethany responds with a bit of a chuckle at her mother-in-law's obvious attempt to interject. "I'll treat." she says. "You know Deborah gives great service, plus, it's a new business. She has been open less than a year, so we are not going to ask for any discounts — as I've told you before. I know what it is like to be in a new business. When I opened my advertising agency, those first few years were scary... I needed all the business and favor I could get."

Bethany gets up from where she is sitting with Sandy and checks on Mama Netty's activity in the kitchen. "Thank God for a mother's prayers... What you cooking, Ma?" Mama Netty has an energetic answer as she commences to recite the morning's menu. "You know what I'm making... My grand-babies getting my homemade biscuits with the butter melting... oozing down the sides... country fried steak, smothered in gravy and eggs. Y'all going to join us?"

Bethany and Sandy each have a look of horror on their faces from the thought of indulging in all those calories. Bethany playfully responds. "We'll pass, ma. Sandy, we better get going if we're going to make this class on time. I don't want Boa to give the class extra push-ups on account of me being late and have everybody giving me the evil eye. Ma, I will be back in a few hours and we can go over the plans for dinner tomorrow." Bethany gathers her workout bag and grabs her keys off the kitchen counter and then her and Sandy disappear out of the door.

In the same moment, Mama Netty's cell phone rings. She quickly pulls it from her robe pocket to answer it, but she handles her phone like a slippery fish out of water and finally brings it to her ears. She missed the call. It rings again, but this time, with a look of satisfaction, she answers the phone, placing the caller on the speaker. A jovial man's voice breaks the morning quietness. "Hello, Netty. How are you doing on this fine morning?"

Mama Netty recognizes the voice and responds, "Oh, just fine, Mr. Thompson. You're up mighty early. You know what's wrong with my car already?" At that very moment, Amber enters the kitchen area from her bedroom. She's wearing a bathrobe and a scarf is tied neatly around her head. Amber begins to listen in as Mr. Thompson answers enthusiastically. "Yes, it's the starter... but not to worry. I'll have it fixed in no time. You know you're one of my pri-or-it-tay customers... ur, uhh... I'll just drop it to you on tomorrow at Bethany's."

Mama Netty quickly objects to Mr. Thompson's generous gesture. "Oh no, Mr. Thompson, don't go through the trouble. It's your weekend. Amber can drop me off at home tomorrow and we can square off on the car sometime on Monday..." Mr. Thompson quickly retorts, cutting her off. "Oh, it's no trouble for me, Netty; besides, isn't there a par-tay happening on tomorrow?" He takes a moment and then proceeds to answer his own question. "See, what we can do is... I can bring your repaired car to you — at no charge to you —ur, uhh — that's the drop off fee... no charge for the drop-off service that is. At any rate ... then, after dinner and when you are ready to go home, you can just drop me off at my place on the way... see... it's all figured out..."

Both Mama Netty and Amber become amused at the current dialogue and struggle to keep their snickering between themselves. "I see Mr. Thompson," Mama Netty answers as she struggles to keep her laugh in check. "You have it all figured out. That will be fine. If you're sure it's not a bother. You know I could get..." He cuts her off again, determined not to miss out on the party. "Not a bother at all... Now, what time is dinner served tomorrow?"

Mama Netty responds, "Right around the three o'clock hour, dinner is served. That's just after church service. Speaking of church, when are we going to see you at church again?" She adds an exaggerated preachy sound for both her and Amber's amusement. "Brother Thompson?" The line is quiet for a few seconds. Mr. Thompson seems to panic at the prospect of a church invite coming his way. "What was that? You seem to be breaking up. This darn phone is acting up again... Ur, I'll see you tomorrow around three o'clock... Okay now, I'll see you later ... Goodbye now."

He thinks he has hung up the phone and begins to talk aloud to himself ... "Got me to lying...Jesus will see me at Christmas service or Easter or the Resurrection service... whatever they call Easter these days... that preacher too long winded for me ... get me to falling asleep... God knows my heart..."

Just then, Mama Netty breaks in to let Mr. Thompson know that he has not disconnected the line. "Brother Thompson... you need to hang up your phone..." With that, Mr. Thompson commences to the same dramatic demonstration he'd put on earlier. "Oh, right. You, um... breaking up...Ur, ummm, goodbye..." The phone goes dead this time. Mama Netty and Amber burst into laughter.

"Mama Netty," Amber chuckles, "You know Mr. Thompson got a crush on you. He invited himself over for the par-tay tomorrow... that's too funny. Man, he always finds some way to spend a little quality time with you. Remember when your air conditioner went out... he found a way to camp out on your sofa for two days... he had to make sure the fans worked properly during the night..."

Mama Netty chimes in on Amber's observation. "You mean, he always finds a way to work me over..." She chuckles to herself and says, "That man was in my way... for two days... he had to fix the shower head, the shower rod, adjust the rugs on the floor, the kitchen sink and the garbage disposal...

the funny thing is … I don't have no garbage disposal… Lord, bless his heart… But you know we love him just the same… you know we the only family he got… really…"

Amber turns her focus to what her grandmother is cooking in the kitchen. "Ma-Netty, what you cooking?" But before she can answer, Amber offers the answer in the same rehearsed voice that her grandmother recited earlier to Bethany. "I know … your famous homemade biscuits with the butter melting… oozing down the sides… country fried steak smothered in gravy and eggs. Ma, you know I love your cooking; you put so much love in it. I hate to break this to you; we don't even eat like that anymore." A disappointed Mama Netty responds to her granddaughter's bad news. "Well, what?! You too young to be trying to watch your figure… I tell you, you teenagers today… but I know this — David Jr. will eat my fried steak and gravy… he'll eat enough for two…"

Their mood changes at the mention of David Jr. They both stare at one another, attempting to console one another. After a few moments of silence, Mama Netty takes Amber in her arms and gives her a comforting hug and then leads her to the sofa where they both sit. Mama Netty begins to console her granddaughter. "It's going to be okay. Whatever it is, it's going to be okay. I don't know what's going on, but I know it's going to be okay. We serve a good God, a merciful God... who cares about us."

Amber answers back in a somber mood, "But, I'm scared... Mama Netty... he's different... he doesn't talk; he barely eats... It just seems like — like he just checked out... all he wants to do is stay locked in his room. Something is not right... and it's been this way for a while... even before our last family dinner, which was more like a family feud..." At this point, David Jr. enters the kitchen area and goes unnoticed by both his sister and grandmother.

Mama Netty continues to share her fears, "I've been watching him... since your father passed... Both of you were such little things when he..." she cuts her sentence short, not able to speak about the painful past. She takes a moment and then continues, "In these past few years... it seems as though he's slowly coming to some sort of reality that he's not willing to accept. He's a lot like your mother you know... they don't handle it well...loss... but your brother... I think there's a tormentor in him...he's so angry..."

Amber breaks in, offering her own opinion as to what is happening to her troubled brother. "Tormentor?!... Yeah... it's called Bethany! All she does is nag at him. That is when she sees him... which is few and far between nowadays. It's like she doesn't even see that something is wrong. Probably because she's hardly ever here... David Jr. is different... he doesn't express his anger in the same way ... and I'm afraid for him, for me... for.... it's like he is the calm before the storm..."

Finally, David Jr. makes his presence known. He interrupts with, "I can hear you." And then leaves as quietly as he entered the kitchen moments earlier. Amber and her grandmother share a startled look at one another as he disappears behind his bedroom door.

Chapter Four

HAPPY BIRTHDAY UNCLE BENNY!

It's Sunday afternoon and the dimly lit dining area is festive with beautiful flowers on the table and a banner hung across the fireplace wall that reads: *Happy Birthday Uncle Benjamin!* David is sitting on the sofa. Nobody else is around and he's softly rocking back and forth as he sits in the dark. Faint voices can be heard outside of the front door and David notices this just before the doorbell chimes break the Sunday afternoon silence. He stops rocking in anticipation of what will happen next.

Moments later, a sleepy and disheveled Bethany, who is a tad bit annoyed, makes her way to the door from her bedroom. She opens the door and in walks the Attaway twins with their arms loaded up with trays of food. None of the women notice David sitting on the sofa in the dark. A festive Cherlene greets Bethany, "Good day to you! We bring good tidings...," and Berlene, finishes the greeting, "... of food for the day's festivities. Happy Birthday, Uncle Benjamin."

A disgruntled Bethany snaps back at them, failing to offer any thanks to the sisters for their good deeds. "Y'all a little loud for it to be so early in the morning... I like to sleep in on Sundays... y'all know this... y'all know you're not right..." Cherlene interrupts Bethany's rant to point out an important fact. She says, "What are you talking about, Bethany? It's 1:30 in the afternoon... Your family will be home in a little bit..."

Berlene is determined to get on with the business that she and her sister came to do, so she says, "Bethany, are you gonna have us working in the dark... can we have some light?" Bethany switches on the lights and David leaps from the couch. He takes an awkward stance in the middle of the living room floor as if he were a soldier at war in the middle of an ambush, imaginary gun drawn in all. The ladies are startled. Bethany yells out, "David Jr!!!"

Nevertheless, no one makes a move as they all stare at David, anticipating his next move. After a moment, he slowly raises his hand and forms his fingers loosely like a gun next to his chin, sort of pointing it at himself and halfway at the ladies. After that, he slowly crosses to his bedroom without saying a word. Chills run down both Berlene and Charlene's spines and they give one another a side-eyed glare. Berlene exclaims, "What the…" as Cherlene finishes her sister's thought, "… just happened!?" An agitated Bethany, who looks to be a little embarrassed, snaps at the sisters. "Just … set up the food; will you? … You know what to do. I've got to jump in the shower."

As Bethany storms off to her bedroom, the sisters burst into laughter, releasing the tension from the moment before. They begin setting up the food trays and putting the last touches on the decorations for the party, all the while, discussing a topic that has become quite popular lately. "There is something strange about David Jr, Cherlene! Something is not right… as I have said one hundred times before … something is not right, and she needs to get him some help before he does some

harm!" And then, she makes a scary face at her
sister before bursting out with more laughter.

Cherlene rebukes her sister. "Berlene, it's not
funny!" Without warning, she also caves into
laughter. By this time, Berlene has her finger in one
of the prepared dishes. "Well, all I have to say is
that the food is good! Let's hope the entertainment
is just as good or better!" They both say at the same
time, "We are staying around for the whole thing!"
With that, they point at one another and shout,
"Jinx!" This is a game they have engaged in every
time they've said the same thing at the same time;
they started this when they were teenagers.

The doorbell chimes ring out and the sisters raise
their voice just loud enough for the person on the
other side of the door to hear them. "It's open; come
in!" Again, they point at one another, shouting "jinx"
in unison. In walks Savannah, Bethany's older sister
and only known living blood relative ... besides her
children. In contrast to Bethany's beauty, refined
charm and class, Savannah is the opposite. Just ten
years Bethany's senior, she appears to be at least
twenty years older. The years of alcohol, drug and

nicotine abuse have taken their toll on her frail body. Only glimpses of her youthful beauty remain, but it is evident that she was likely as beautiful as Bethany at some point in her life. Her shoulder length dark curls are loosely worn and are in bad need of a good trim and a color treatment. Years of sun damage and premature graying have taken their toll on her once beautiful head of hair. But it is Savannah's dark apathetic eyes that tell the story of a woman who gave up on living life to its fullest years ago.

"Well, stop staring at me as if you've seen a ghost; Mama Netty insisted that I come." The sisters greet Savannah with one voice. "Well, hello!" Again, they point at one another and shout, "Jinx!" Berlene suddenly pulls a crisp twenty-dollar bill out of her pocket and grudgingly slaps it into Cherlene's open hand. "Oh, I see..." Savannah says as she realizes the sins of the twins. "Y'all making bets on me. Well, how y'all doing, Ms. Cherlene and Berlene?" She attempts to insult them as they have done to her. "The old maids that live next door. The busy body twins... that don't even look alike... how that happen... I still don't know..."

Offended, Berlene snaps back at her and says, "We are fraternal twins; we keep telling you!" Savannah bites back. "You mean fra-scandal twins; don't you? Always in business that don't belong to you... but I bet the food is good... nothing like good food to go along with good drama... right?! She uncovers one of the dishes of food sitting on the table, sticks her index finger into the food and then places her finger in her mouth. "Ummm ... good." The sisters have a horrified look on their faces and they briefly look at one another, wondering how Bethany's sister has managed to know their secrets.

She chuckles at them both and switches her mood to that of a playful one, bringing relief to the moment. "How y'all doing? You know I'm just messing with you. You got any good gossip on the whereabouts of my ever-effervescent sister?" The twins begin to breathe again, and with a sigh of relief, Berlene answers her with a bit of a warning in her voice. "She's in there... taking a shower and will be out in a minute," she says as she points to Bethany's bedroom door. Savannah is not moved by the possibility of encountering Bethany and heads towards David's bedroom. "I know my niece is at church, but where is my nephew?" She disappears behind his bedroom door.

Just then, Bethany reappears from her bedroom wrapped in a plushy robe but with her hair and makeup done. The Attaway twins have a look of horror on their faces and both refuse to say a word. Bethany begins her morning ritual of vitamin taking and then pours a cup of coffee for herself before heading back into her bedroom. Berlene and Cherlene begin to nibble from one of the food trays. Once again, they say in unison, "This is getting ready to get really good!" Once again, they point at one another and shout, "Jinx!"

The doorbell chimes and again, the twins answer in the same manner as before. "It's open; come on in!" Again, they point at one another and shout, "Jinx!" Moments later, in walks Uncle Benjamin, dressed in his Sunday's best. He immediately walks over to the twins and looks at one of them first and then the other. "Well, hello there. Is it Cherlene or Berlene? Which is it? You know I can never tell you two apart."

They look at one another in amusement. Then Berlene speaks. She answers, "Hello Uncle Ben. Glad to see you made it in okay. How long you going to be in our neck of the woods?" He answers without noticing that he didn't get an answer to his previous question. "Oh, I guess I'm going to be around until at least Thanksgiving. I've decided to stick around for a while for this visit. Where is everyone? Bethany home?"

Berlene answers, "Yes, they are at church — except for Bethany. She's in her room and will be out in a minute and…" She points towards David's room, but he cuts her off. "Okay, well I'm going to hurry up to get settled in and freshen up before they get in from church. That spare room at the end of the hallway is not occupied… do you know?" Berlene gives her best answer, "I don't think so…but…" He cuts her off again, eager to get settled in. "Alright then. I will see you ladies in a few." He points at them while reciting their names and gets them mixed up again.

As he disappears down the hallway, Savannah reappears from David's room and she crosses to the kitchen area talking to herself. "What did they do to my nephew?! Something is not right with him. I could tell as soon as I laid my eyes on him. Has she even done anything for him…" A fully dressed Bethany enters from her bedroom with her coffee in her hand and stops dead in her steps. Meanwhile, the Attaway twins have settled in as if they are in front row seats at a good stage play in anticipation of what will happen.

Savannah continues to rant, not noticing her sister's presence. "Take him to the doctor somebody! Something is on his mind… I know sickness when I see it… trouble…" Bethany cuts her short. "Who let her in here? What is she doing in here?" She then turns and speaks directly to Savannah. "Why are you here? You know you are not welcome in my house. I thought I made myself clear about that. I don't have time for some good for nothing… trash… that don't want to do nothing but blame others for their drama… you…"

Savannah, who is not moved or intimidated by Bethany's rage, cuts her little sister off. "Bethany, please… stop with all the drama cause you are the drama queen. It's not even about all that... we can have a peaceful..." Bethany is now even more disturbed as she raises her voice over her sister's.

"Get out my house, Savannah! I don't want you here, not around my children; you are not welcome. You come in here already starting stuff. I heard you. You're the one that needs a doctor cause your head is all messed up! Sickness! Of course, you know sickness; you see it every day... when you wake up and look at yourself... How dare you!"

Bethany points to the door and shouts at the top of her lungs. "GET OUT!" Savannah, obviously drunk, begins to taunt her sister. She raises her hands in front of her and her mouth is wide open as she begins to move like a zombie. She takes a few steps toward Bethany and abruptly stops and lets her eyeballs roll to the back of her head. Bethany gets so frustrated that she violently throws the coffee mug that she has in her hand at Savannah and barely misses her. It splashes and crashes to the floor and the Attaway twins scurry to clean it up.

Amber and Mama Netty enter through the front door, laughing and talking, oblivious to the violent moment before. "Well look here, Amber! Savannah has graced us with her presence. Hello..." Mama Netty notices the tension in Savannah's face and realizes Bethany is standing nearby. Amber, who notices the look on Bethany's face intervenes. "Okay, what just happened?" Bethany, not taking her eyes off Savannah, answers her daughter, "Your auntie was just leaving."

Mama Netty takes Savannah by the hand and motions to Amber to follow as she leads them to the sofa. The Attaway twins have settled in the kitchen area to look on as they each nibble from one of the platters of food. "Nonsense," Mama Netty says to Bethany. "She just got here... Now what we all need to do is to just take a moment and settle down. Let's start this afternoon off on the right note... It's not often that we get to come together ..." Just as soon as the three get settled on the sofa, Mama Netty leaps to her feet with excitement, eager to greet Uncle Benjamin, her son, as he appears from down the hallway.

"Well looky here, looky here! When did you arrive? Well come on over here and say hello! Oh, it's going to be a good day!" Uncle Benjamin greets his mother with a big bear hug, says his "hellos" both to Bethany and Savannah and immediately turns his attention to Amber, his niece. "Amber... you are so precious; look at you. You growing up so fast..." Falling into his arms, Amber returns an affectionate hug and greeting to her uncle. "Uncle Benny, you say that every time... it's only been a few months since you've seen me last. How are you doing? You're looking well yourself." The two of them take seats on the couch as the doorbell chimes ring out.

Mama Netty immediately starts for the door. "That could be the Pastors; I told them about three p.m. for dinner..." She nervously barks orders first to the Attaway twins. "Is dinner ready to be served? Get the table ready; will you?" After that, Mama Netty turns to Bethany and issues her a stern warning. "Mind your manners..." She opens the door and greets Pastors Wynn and Mary Charleston in her warmest charming voice. "Well, come on in Pastors; you are right on time. We are just about ready to take our seats at the table and have you to bless the food. Amen!"

She turns to everyone with a bit of nervous energy. "Everyone, say hello to our new pastors — Pastors Wynn and Mary Charleston." As she leads the couple to the dining area, she begins to acquaint them with her family. "You know Amber, of course, and Bethany; and have you met Bethany's sister, Savannah? Now, this is my son, Benjamin, but you have met him also... yes, well you know everyone... uhh, Amber, go get your brother, David Jr. We about ready to eat."

Amber jumps from her seat next to her Uncle Benjamin and starts for her brother's room as the pastors begin to exchange greetings with everyone. The Attaway sisters continue to hustle about, bringing the food to the table, as well as the other preparations. Savannah makes her way over to Uncle Benjamin on the couch, as Bethany greets the pastors with one eye and threatens her sister with her other eye. Mama Netty is busy being the best host she can possibly be. She briefly oversees the dinner table activity and then chats with the pastors for a moment. Afterward, she gives a look of warning to Bethany and goes back to the table to make sure everything is set to her liking.

The frenetic energy comes to an abrupt standstill as the doorbell chimes ring out just one more time. In the next moment, all eyes are on Mr. Thompson, who doesn't wait for an invitation, but bursts through the doors, commanding the floor. "Hello, hello, hello everyone. How is everyone doing on this fine Sunday afternoon? Is it time to eat...?" He is getting ready to cut up with his best comic relief but notices the pastors and instead, changes his tune. He greets them with his most holy voice. "Hello Pastor. Amen, amen. Now, you going to see me at church soon..."

Just then, Amber and a disgruntled David comes to join everyone as they all begin to migrate toward the dinner table. Bethany corrects her son with a whisper, but everyone can hear her. "David Jr, pull up your pants... looking like a rough rider. Where is your belt?!" Amber quickly comes to her brother's rescue as she whispers out of embarrassment to her mother. "Ma, leave him alone, come on..."

Mama Netty commands the floor. She breaks in to get the serving of dinner underway. She says, "Mr. Thompson, you are just in time. We are ready to gather at the table. Now take your hat off and come join us. Everyone stands behind a chair at the dining room table except for the Attaway sisters, who make their seats not far away at the kitchen counter as they serve the family. As everyone settles, Mama Netty gives instructions to the pastor. "Pastor Wynn, please do us the honor of blessing us, the table and the food with one of your beautiful prayers."

Pastor Wynn takes over with reverential authority. "Let us all bow our heads in reverence of the Father, who has blessed us with all things pertaining to life and godliness. Dear heavenly Father, we join together this afternoon due to our faith in you. We ask you to bless us with your presence as we fellowship with one another. We ask for virtue, Father. Let our faith be enough to show brotherly love, gentleness and kindness toward one another as we partake of this feast. Bless this house where we sit and give peace to the one who has opened her house for this occasion.

Bless the hands who have prepared this food. Now, Lord, we ask you to bless the food, as you have provided so abundantly. As we eat, we claim healing for mind, body and soul as you have promised to bless our food and water and to take sickness away from the midst of us. We pray for these things and all things in the name of Jesus. Amen."

Everyone repeats in unison, "Amen" and begins to take their seats. Amber, looks to her Uncle with joy in her heart as she states the reason for the occasion. "Well, Uncle Benny... Happy birthday! The Attaway sisters have finalized their duties of serving the table and as they take their seats at the kitchen counter, they look at one another and speak in unison, "Let the games begin..." They then point to one another and say, "Jinx!"

Chapter Five

PRAYER ANTIDOTES AND AFTER DINNER ANTICS

In the two hours during dinner and up until now, the Clearwater family managed to hold their peace with one another. The family and friends are now sitting in the family room partaking in small talk, coffee and birthday cake. However, the atmosphere has begun to get a little tense. Savannah appears to be a bit tipsier than when the evening began and though Bethany has been sitting with Pastor Mary, she has managed to find ways to agitate her sister.

David is sitting off to himself in a state of what looks like a deep hypnotic trance and Amber is frustrated because no one seems to notice. Mama Netty, Uncle Benjamin, Mr. Thompson and Pastor Wynn have a deep spiritual conversation going on, though it's arguable if Mr. Thompson is even paying attention. The Attaway sisters are busy putting the leftover food away, cleaning dishes and tidying up the kitchen.

Pastor Wynn is the first to break up the party as he stands to his feet to make his announcement. "We are going to have to be heading home now. Uncle Benny, happy birthday to you once again. Since you are going to be with us for a while, don't be a stranger at church on Sundays." He turns his attention to Mr. Thompson next. "Mr. Thompson, Christmas and Resurrection Sunday are not the only two Sundays in the year. We hope to see you soon... in the meantime, we are praying for you, brother."

Pastor Mary rises to her feet to express her appreciation for the evening and to join her husband. "Yes, we want to thank you for this lovely evening and scrumptious food. It certainly has been a treat for us tonight. Berlene and Cherlene, you'll have to give me that recipe for those divine potatoes."

She turns to Bethany, whips out a business card from her handbag, and says "Keep my office hours in mind and call me if you need anything at all; here is my card. Do you mind if we pray for you and the family before we leave?" Mama Netty interjects, "Not at all! I was just thinking the same. Come on everyone; let's gather around for prayer. Thank you, Pastor, for offering."

They all rise and form a circle and Pastors Wynn and Mary stand in the center. Pastor Wynn takes the lead, "Let's bow our heads. Lord, we thank you for making your presence known here this evening. Thank you for this family. We ask you to continue to bless them. Meet them wherever they are in need, whether it be a financial need, physical need of healing, psychological, mental, emotional or circumstantial. We ask that you pour out your choice blessings upon each of them. Forgive our sins and trespasses against you and one another so that we may find favor with you."

He then goes and puts his hands on both of Uncle Benjamin's shoulders and begins to bless him. "Let this be the most significant birthday year he has had yet. We know there are no coincidences in you; there is purpose in you bringing him here to his family at this time. Whatever is needed and however you desire to use him to be a blessing to his family, let it be so."

Pastor Mary instinctively goes and stands before Savannah, and in the same manner as her husband, begins to pray. "Lord, help this life. We know that you have a good plan and not an evil plan for her. We pray that you would intervene. We ask you to convince her of your love so much so that any guilt, shame or unworthiness loses its strength over her. We speak deliverance and healing over this life now, in Jesus name."

Pastor Wynn takes over as he prays over David Jr., laying his hand upon David's head, "O Lord, our God. Again, we speak your Word over your son. Before you placed him in his mother's belly, you knew him. We say that your original plans, purposes and will for his life shall not be altered. We stand against any generational curses or any familiar spirits from the underworld at work against his life. God, only you know what is needed for this life to be sustained in your perfect peace. We claim that wholeness now in Jesus name."

And again, Pastor Mary takes over praying a perfect prayer for Bethany. "God, let this be a season of deliverance from the old. I declare renewal, restoration and revival in this life. As we approach this season of Thanksgiving, let Bethany know all that she has to be grateful for. We pray, Father, that you continue to work for her good in all things. Give her the true abundant life. Amen."

Pastor Wynn begins to close the prayer, but then goes over to Mr. Thompson and gives him certain instructions. "Yes, Lord... Brother Thompson, just say, "Yes Lord!" Mr. Thompson pops open his eyes with surprise and with a comical look of fear on his face, he seems to be at a loss for words. Pastor Wynn gives him the same instruction. "Just say it with me, "Yes Lord! Say it, brother!"

Mr. Thompson seems to have a problem getting the words out. He stutters, meanwhile everyone in the prayer circle looks to be routing for him to say it. Finally, after a few stutters, a hearty, "Yes, Lord!" spills out of Mr. Thompson's mouth. The on-lookers spontaneously cheer for him as several "amen" and "hallelujahs" are heard. Pastor Wynn's voice can be heard amidst the celebration as he concludes the prayer for the evening. "Father, bring him back to church and cause him to fall in love with your will. Order his steps and we pray all these things in Jesus Name. Amen."

"Well goodnight to you all. Once again, thanks for having us... it's been...real!" They all begin to show gratitude to the pastors for the prayer and Mama Netty and Amber walk with them out of the door and to their car. The Attaway sisters resume tidying up the kitchen, Mr. Thompson plops down on a chair, needing a moment to recover from the pressure placed on him by the prayer and David Jr. makes his escape into his bedroom.

Almost immediately, Bethany resumes the argument she had with her sister before dinner. She goes and stands in front of Savannah, who is sitting on the sofa with Uncle Ben, and starts right in with an aggressive tone, "So Savannah, you can get your stuff together and get going now. It's still early. You can safely make it to a bus stop and get on to your favorite watering hole."

Savannah may be a bit frail in stature compared to Bethany, but she makes up for it in attitude. In a casual tone, she barks right back at Bethany, refusing to be intimidated or shamed. "Bethany, get out my face. Move now... I pay you no mind! I'm going to continue to visit with my family until I'm finished... and when I'm ready to go, then I will go."

The Attaway twins take their seats on cue to get a good view of what's getting ready to happen. They briefly look at one another and grin. It appears that Mr. Thompson needed a nap since he can be seen slumped over on the couch with his eyes closed and a faint snoring sound can be heard coming from him. Nevertheless, Uncle Benjamin is determined to intervene between the two sisters.

Uncle Benjamin, is a gentle soul — one who seeks peace and gets very uncomfortable with confrontations, especially when conflict arises between those whom he loves. His family sees him as their very own gentle giant. Standing an impressive 6'7" and weighing in at or around three hundred pounds, he rises and gently puts his hand on Bethany's shoulder before speaking. "Bethany, let's try to get along tonight. It's not often that we have an opportunity to come together as a family; besides, it's my birthday!"

Bethany refuses to back down — not even for Uncle Benjamin. "Sorry, I don't want to hear it tonight, Uncle Ben. She's got to go! She cannot stay in this house." She turns to Savannah once again and locks eyes with her sister before pointing to the door for a more dramatic effect. "Get up and get going... you deadbeat!"

Savannah, who is too tipsy to be offended at Bethany's name-calling, reaches in her handbag and brings out a small bottle of whiskey. Without taking her mischievous eyes off Bethany, she unscrews the cap and commences to drink from the bottle. Bethany becomes enraged and snatches the bottle and handbag out of Savannah's lap. Savannah springs to her feet and with great force, gives Bethany a shove. The force is so great that Bethany stumbles across the room trying to regain her footing, but finally falls on her backside, landing right in front of the door at Amber and Mama Netty's feet.

"What is going on here?" Mama Netty stands towering over Bethany with her hands on her hips, first looking at Bethany and then to Savannah. She then continues her admonishment to them both. "Is this the way we're going to end the evening? You both ought to be ashamed of yourselves. No sooner than the pastors close in prayer and before they can even leave the driveway…y'all at it."

Savannah comes to her own defense. "Because Bethany is just so evil, Netty… but she is going to mess around and get some bodily injury and her little feelings hurt… she don't know how to hold her tongue… I don't know how to hold my tongue either." She scours at Bethany, and if looks could kill, she would have murdered her sister with a glance. Savannah, still looking intently at Bethany yells out, "It's getting ready to get deep up in here!"

As she picks herself off the floor, Bethany starts towards Savannah, but Amber steps in front of her mother. Bethany begins to shout at Savannah while trying to step around Amber. "This is my house, Savannah. I own this house, my property, my stuff… I shouldn't have to tell you but once to get up on out of here! Look around," Bethany says as she randomly points to items in her house. "My furniture, my sofa, my table... my children... my in-laws. Why are you here? Get up and go; get your own life!"

Mama Netty has heard enough, so she shouts, "Bethany! You two stop it; stop this now!" But Savannah continues. "I feel sorry for you, Bethany... you got some serious issues. You think you all that. You don't have it going on. You know that; right!? I mean, you are so ungrateful. As much as I've done for you... you know when I had it together, I would've done anything for you..."

Bethany is amused at her sister's comments and counters with, "Excuse me — but when did you ever have it together? I did this. When did you help me?" Savannah becomes indignant at these last statements. "I got a job and gave you money here and there. I bought you a coat." Bethany laughs at her sister's comments. "Unbelievable!!! Some pocket change and a coat?" The rest of the family tries to get Bethany to calm down and to be quiet, but the sisters seem to be in a bitter world all by themselves as they go back and forth with one another. "It was all I had... and you needed that coat!"

Bethany talks over her older sister, determined to make it all about her. "I managed to graduate college, get my degree, get married, and have my children... I did this, Savannah! I built my business... I pulled myself up by my own bootstraps... look around... I built this..." Savannah is fed up with Bethany's self-centered attitude and she finally breaks. She doesn't even seem to be tipsy anymore.

"Yep, everybody look... This is it... the house that Bethany built... and I just wonder when it's all going to shatter and come tumbling down..." She deliberately looks at her sister and says, "You do know pride does come before a fall; don't you? ... Will you be bragging bout what you accomplished then? Please, this house is built on nothing but glass ... hypocrisy... you sit up talking all nice and holy to that lady pastor... now you are bragging bout your children... you don't see that something is desperately wrong with your son. Look inside the house you've built, Bethany, and look for a mirror

so you can see that you've made it all about you!"
Savannah reaches for her empty liquor bottle on
the floor. "You wouldn't be acting like this if David
Sr. was still alive..."

This last statement of Savannah's hits a nerve with
Bethany and she goes after her sister, shouting,
"Don't you dare put my husband's name on your
lips!" The sisters are now locked in a shouting and
shoving match with one another and the family
members try to break them up. There is so much
chaos that no one notices when David Jr. enters the
family room with an empty look on his face. There
is a loud guttural scream and the sound of a
handgun cocking. The family is startled to silence as
they look towards the sounds and they quickly see
that David Jr. is brandishing a handgun, pointing it
at himself, and at times, at various members of the
family.

Uncle Benjamin immediately tries to approach
David to rescue the gun from his hands, but to no
avail since David turns the gun on his uncle and
sternly warns him not to come any closer. "Son,"
Uncle Benjamin pleads with his nephew, "You don't

want to hurt yourself or anyone else..." Next, Mama Netty pleads with David with all the loving grandmother affection she can possibly muster up. "David, calm down, son. Baby please put the gun down."

David waves the gun as he shouts, "Stand back... stay away from me! You don't know. You don't know what I want to do... I know what I want ...He knew what he wanted to do to!" Bethany clearly does not take her son seriously and she impatiently approaches him with an attitude. "What are you talking about, David? Who are you talking about?" David, snaps back at his mother, while turning the gun towards her. "You know who I'm talking about... My father, David Sr.! He knew what he wanted to do... I saw; it was not an accident... He meant it! He knew what he wanted... He didn't want me... He wanted to leave!"

An irritated Bethany continues to reason with her son. "David Jr., now, you just talking nonsense... put that gun down and straighten up; I mean it! This approach only causes David to become more frantic. He begins to shout and threaten her again with the gun. "I saw him. I know what I saw. I always knew what I saw. You tried to make me forget... but I know... I'm not crazy... I saw him..."

Uncle Benjamin tries to intervene again as he reasons with his nephew. "David, son, of course you saw. You found the body and you were just a little boy. I know that had to be horrible for you, son. We can work through this. Are you ready to talk about it?" David Jr. screams at his uncle, "I just didn't find my father's dead body; I saw him..."

Mama Netty is horrified with disbelief as she listens to her grandson. "Are you suggesting that he...?" She can't bring herself to say what she is coming to realize, so David finishes the thought. "Killed himself... yes, he killed himself..." His body begins to shake as he sobs, tears are streaming down his face as he continues to purge from the secret that he has kept for too long. "He didn't want me so he killed himself... He took the gun and killed himself... I was there." He finds the strength to raise the gun to his own head again. "Now, I'm just like my father. I don't want you."

He puts on a determined face and the family panics as they anticipate what will happen next. Everyone feels the intensity of the moment. There is a dreaded silence and everything appears to be moving in slow motion as he places the gun directly against his temple and pulls the trigger. There is silence... no bullet, and with a sigh of relief, a few of the family members start moving towards him. Again, he threatens them with the gun. "I do have bullets in here, so stay back..."

He begins to wave the gun erratically, then randomly at one family member after the other. They clinch with fear as the gun is pointed at each of them. The Attaway twins have barricaded themselves in the kitchen, their eyes peeking just enough over the marbled counter-top to ensure they don't miss out on the excitement of the night. Unbelievably, Mr. Thompson has slept through all the commotion. He has remained on the couch in the same awkward sleeping position.

Amber and Savannah have found a semi-safe place to stand. They are embracing and comforting one another as they observe in shock, disbelief and desperation. Bethany is on the opposite side of the room with her arms folded one over the other. Her attitude is much different from the others. First, she doesn't believe for a minute that there are bullets in the gun and second, that there is anything wrong with her son. She believes that this is just another way for him to command attention and to torture her.

Lastly, she's wondering when someone is going to get the notion to take the gun away so that the family can get on with their lives. Uncle Benjamin and Mama Netty are the heroes for the evening. They are each standing on opposite sides of David, inching their way closer and closer, hoping to calm him enough to overtake him. Their mission is to get both David and the family out of harm's way.

However, David Jr. continues to hold the two at bay as he wildly wields the gun. He continues to cleanse himself of the emotional trauma he's held in for so long. For the first time since witnessing his father's death, with great tears and sobs, he begins to tell his story. "He didn't see me...He told me to stay away from his tools. I didn't want to get into trouble, so when I heard him at the door of the garage, I hid on the other side of the car. He didn't see me." He begins to punish himself by hitting the top of his head with the gun. "I should've said something; I should've told him that I was there... then he wouldn't have done it... but I saw him..."

And then, the look on David's face reveals that he is suddenly realizing something, something that has eluded him in times past. "... and he saw me... It happened so fast... He had the gun. I saw from the side mirror of the car. I didn't know what he was getting ready to do or else I would have saved him... I could have saved him, you know... but I didn't know when he got the gun what he was planning to do..." He takes a moment to wipe his face and then continues to share his story. "I was just a little boy... I saw him raise the gun... through the mirror... I knew and I ran from behind the car to save him... but he pulled the trigger... and he saw me... he saw me... but he had already pulled the trigger; it was too late... but he saw me... I think, I think... he was sorry he pulled the trigger..., but I couldn't tell because it was so quick. His eyes and my eyes... I can't get it out of my head... I saw him... ... He saw me..."

The pain of reenacting the horrible moment that he locked eyes with his father just before he took his life shows on David's face. The thought of the guilt this child has been carrying inside is overwhelming for the family as Mama Netty, Uncle Benjamin, Savannah and Amber begin to sob. Even the Attaway sisters are tearful. Bethany continues to stand with her arms folded one over the other, and the only sign of her being affected is that of a stone face.

Now that his story is out of him, David Jr. finally breaks and puts down the gun. The family, except for Bethany, runs to his rescue. Amber arrives first and scoops up the gun. The rest of the family gathers around David, embracing and consoling him. Meanwhile, Amber tinkers with the gun and it goes off, making a loud sound and firing into a wall, barely missing Bethany. Startled by the sound of the gun, Mr. Thompson suddenly awakens and leaps to his feet, shouting, "Happy New Year!" There is an eerie quiet as the family stares at Bethany and then at the hole in the wall just above her head.

Chapter Six

ALL ABOUT DAVID SR.

One week later on a Saturday afternoon, Mr. Thompson is busy working on repairing the wall with the bullet hole. Uncle Benjamin is sipping on a cup of coffee and keeping him company. Amber is busy working on her laptop on the sofa. Uncle Benjamin is in a nostalgic mood as he reflects on the past. "Here's another wall in this house with a bullet hole. I wonder how much more this house can take. If these walls could talk... humph ... they would have some stories to tell. I remember when this house was being built. David, my brother — my baby brother — couldn't settle for a house that was already built. No way! He had big dreams, high hopes and the smarts to pull them all off. His famous phrase was, "I'm going to have my pie in the sky, right here on Earth in the NOW!"

Mama Netty, who has just entered from the bedroom area joins the conversation. "Lord! How many times did we hear that?! That David wasn't going to settle for nothing in life... He was barely twelve when he turned that $150 he earned from his paper route into nine thousand dollars. He did this all by himself, trading on that E-trade from his computer." She chuckles at the thought as she utters, "He wasn't even in high school and was already planning for his retirement."

Amber looks up from her laptop. "What?! I never knew that about Daddy." Uncle Benjamin answers, beaming in pride for his little brother. He says, "Yeah, things seemed to come pretty easy for little David." Mr. Thompson interrupts, "Forgive me for saying, but you know, for him to be adopted and all... he didn't miss a beat." Mama Netty thinks back to that time as she tries to remember his age. "By the time he had come to us, he was just turning seven or was it eight? I don't think he was nine yet..."

Uncle Benjamin confidently confirms his age. "I remember; he was turning eight, because I had just turned eighteen and was headed off to college." He smiles to himself. "I have to admit, I was a little worried about leaving you alone, but it wasn't long after he arrived that I knew everything would be okay... the way y'all took to one another."

Mama Netty begins to shake her head in agreement as she continues to remember those earlier days. "Yes, by that time, he had already been in the foster care system for five years and a few houses. I couldn't understand who wouldn't want this little boy. From the time I laid my eyes on him, I knew that he was something special... he was peculiar... in a good way."

Uncle Benjamin slightly changes the subject and asks, "He was the reason you got back into the church; wasn't he, Mama?" She confirms this fact by nodding her head in affirmation. She then chuckles to herself adding, "Yes, he was the reason for a lot of changes. You remember that Friday night, Mr. Thompson, you were with us." Mr. Thompson knows exactly what Netty is talking about, so he just continues her vein of thinking. "Me, you and everyone else in the neighborhood... that little boy had a way of persuading you... Just about the whole neighborhood in church on a Friday night?!"

Mama Netty gets energized as she delights in sharing with her granddaughter and remembering those good times with David Sr. "He was determined to win that bicycle prize. He had to have the most guests attend the closing night of VBS ..." Then, she has a more serious moment, "... but when it was time for altar call and I got a glimpse of the look on that little boy's face as he went to the altar... I knew there was something genuine going on with him and God. More than just the bicycle prize, he received something real on that day... I made up in mind that whatever it was, I was going to do everything in my power to make sure he kept it."

Mr. Thompson suddenly laughs and breaks the seriousness of the moment as he comes to a sudden realization. "Oh, is that why you stopped drinking and coming around for the Friday night card parties?" Amber is both surprised and amused at this bit of information about her grandmother. "Mama Netty, you used to drink... and play cards...?" Mr. Thompson quickly adds the rest of the untold story, "... and smoke and cuss and..."

Mama Netty quickly cuts him short of spilling all the beans about her sordid past. "Hush now, Mr. Jerry Thompson! You telling all my business to my grand-baby!" She laughs and looks at her granddaughter. "Amber don't need to know that I wasn't born in Holy Ghost diapers!" She gets animated for a moment as she pantomimes playing a heated card game as if she throws the winning hand on the card table and they all laugh. Mama Netty cuts into their laughter with another thought directed at Amber. She says, "But your daddy almost was..."

Amber has a puzzled look on her face as Mama Netty continues, "...born in Holy Ghost diapers... from the time he went to that altar on that Friday night, he prospered... in everything. God was just on him... we attended church faithfully. He excelled in school, got good grades... found favor with his teachers."

Mama Netty has a moment of appreciation for David Sr. "He was not a hard case. He was a joy... he changed my life. By the time he got into high school, he knew what he wanted and went after it..." Uncle Benjamin cuts in and says, "He was going to be a banker... and a banker he became... and he kept God in the picture." Bethany enters through the front door as Mama Netty notices what Amber is pointing to on her laptop. "What's that?" Mama Netty squints her eyes to read it out loud. "Etrade.com." Amber playfully announces her current inspiration as she nudges her grandmother. "I want to be like my daddy." They all begin to laugh again.

Bethany breaks the mood with a cold voice. "Your daddy is dead. According to your brother, he killed himself." With this, Amber snaps her laptop shut, jumps to her feet and storms out of the room. Mr. Thompson begins to gather his tools and supplies as he takes Bethany's arrival as a cue for his departure. "Well, that about does it!" He catches himself and changes his tone. "I mean, for this wall. It's repaired. Bethany, I will send you the bill." He shows himself out of the front door as quickly as he gathered his tools. Mama Netty and Uncle Benjamin look at Bethany and both are trying to hide their annoyance. "What y'all looking at?!" Bethany asks with a flippant attitude.

Mama Netty decides to ignore her daughter in-law's faults to inquire about her grandson. "How is David Jr.? What are the doctors saying?" Before Bethany can answer, Uncle Benjamin inquires as well. "When can we see him? It's been over a week already." Bethany stares at them both and then, in a casual manner, proceeds to answer. "You can start visiting him beginning today, but he won't be there long cause there is nothing wrong with David Jr. He's just trying to get attention as he always has. Soon, the doctors will realize that and you will too. He's so dramatic; he didn't get that from me."

Mama Netty has come to the end of her patience with Bethany. "Bethany... what happened to you? You are so dark-hearted." Bethany cuts through the tension with a rapid answer. "What happened to me?! Really? You can stand there and ask that?! You were there. You both were there. Let's see... I'm a widow; my husband died, leaving me with two small children to raise... by myself... and debt... a whole lot of debt."

Mama Netty strongly objects to this last comment and comes to her dead son's defense. "You had an insurance policy..." Bethany quickly responds, "Which got me through for a few years. We lost a whole lot of money and assets in that stock market crash. It was like starting over. I had nothing, but an insurance policy from a dead husband... who got to check out and leave me with two children, a big beautiful house to keep up with, no income and a whole lot of debt!"

The three are silent for a moment and then, Bethany finally speaks up again; this time, she is a little calmer. "David Sr. is what happened to me. The love of my life, the one I thought I'd grow old with deserted me. The one who said that he was ready to go through hell and high water with me... and for me... hell and high water came, and what did he do?!"

Uncle Benjamin offers an excuse which sends Bethany into a bit of a rage again. She shouts, "You and I both know that there was no gunshot wound to the neck accident on this property eight years ago... I went along with the report. I was relieved when the coroner ruled David Sr.'s death an accident, but deep down, I knew he had ... He was a weak man... and I didn't know that about him. I really didn't know that."

There is a moment of silence before Bethany reiterates what she's already stated earlier. "David Sr. is what happened to me." Mama Netty takes a deep breath as she prepares to have a long-awaited conversation with Bethany. "Bethany, there's a lot you don't understand... He wasn't weak. My David wasn't weak. I believe there is a devil in hell..." Bethany responds to Mama Netty with a bit of sarcasm in her voice, "Ohhhhh, the devil made him do it."

Mama Netty patiently continues to explain. "When trouble came, David just wasn't ready for the battle; it caught him off guard. He was seeing a psychiatrist and he was getting a grip on his diagnosis of mental illness. I told him to talk to you — to tell you — that you could take it. He said that he wasn't ready to accept that diagnosis — that God would rescue him as He always had, and that telling you would be like admitting he had it. But when the stock market crashed and he lost so much..."

Bethany cuts back with venomous sarcasm in her voice. She interjects, "Well, that's it... that's the reason he lost... it wasn't God's fault after all. He didn't give me a chance." She looks at Mama Netty to make sure she is heard. "I'm the fighter; all my life I've had to fight... through school, through my childhood, through college. He should've gotten the revelation... I was the fighter! Everything came easy for him — that was a blessing, but it didn't come so easy for me ... I knew how to fight and I would've helped him fight. He didn't give me a chance... things would've gotten better ... see! Look around; look around, David Sr.! Things got better... I still have my house, my children... when the going got tough, I started a business... successful business ... I didn't check out ...See what good of a fighter I am, David Sr.! Well, you should've trusted me, instead of God."

Mama Netty compassionately interjects and says, "Bethany, don't say that..." Uncle Benjamin interrupts with rebuke in his tone. "Bethany! Have some respect for the dead and God... you don't know what you are saying..." Bethany cuts him off, ignoring his advice and then, responds to what Mama Netty said. "Don't say what, Mama Netty? That God will let you down?" She begins to Mock David Sr. "I want to raise my children in the Lord," he would say. "God is good ... I'm blessed and highly favored. Well, what did it get him? I'll tell you what it got him: mental illness and some fatherless children. Where is he now?! Six feet under..." She looks up towards Heaven and shouts, "Well, David Sr., I guess you have your 'pie in the sky' now!"

Uncle Benjamin is determined to change Bethany's thinking. "Bethany. Now, you gotta let go of all this bitterness at David Sr., at God, and ... you got to look around you and see what all you have to be grateful for." But Bethany is unwilling to be changed, so she responds to his wisdom with more sarcasm and self-exaltation. "I am grateful! I'm grateful to me... because I did this. God didn't do nothing for me."

She pridefully tilts her head back, and with a bit of cockiness in her words, she asks, "Where was He when I was fighting my way out of debt — fighting my way out of foreclosure? So, you can keep on trusting God. Mama Netty, I let you keep taking my children to that church because I like you and I know you love your grandchildren, but give credit where credit is due. I did this! ... And... where is God now?"

Bethany takes a seat on the couch and there is a spirit of sadness that comes flooding into the living room. She lowers her head, sinks her shoulders and folds her hands in her lap. She shows a different kind of emotion as she continues, "I have to fight ... I have to fight my son out of mental illness." Bethany looks defeated as she breaks down and sobs. Amber, who has been listening to the conversation, bursts into the room and demands information from her mom. "What's wrong with David Jr.?"

There is no answer, but Amber is determined to get a response. "Mom." Bethany wipes the tears from her eyes, pulls herself together and finds her voice again to answer her daughter. "The doctors say he is bi-polar and maybe schizophrenic." Mama Netty jumps to her feet, determined to act. "Benjamin, grab your jacket; Amber, get my bag... we are going to David Jr. As God is my witness, this thing shall not be!"

Chapter Seven

GIRL TALK AND LADIES NIGHT

The following Thursday evening, Amber and Wendy enter the house through the front door. They are in deep conversation. As they instinctively walk over to the couch to rest themselves, Wendy tries to win her friend's support. They lower their bags as Wendy continues her dialogue.

"Look, Amber, I just want you to be happy for me. We are dating now and I think he might be the one..."

"The one what, Wendy?" Amber becomes animated and counters with, "The one as in the one? ... Y'all have been dating for less than a week, Wendy."

Wendy ignores Amber's objections and tries to start a different line of questioning. "So, tell me again... why don't you think he's the right man for me? I mean, look, he still has my pictures on his Facebook page...and look at this — one of both of us."

Amber rolls her eyes at her friend. "Wendy... that's you photobombing." Amber giggles at her friend, but when she realizes her friend is not in a laughing mood, she changes her tone to that of a more serious one. "Wendy, I've given you all the reasons I can think of and you're still trying to debate me. What?! Are you trying to convince yourself still? ... And just because he hasn't deleted your pictures off his wall does not mean you've met the perfect man... He's a playa... a wolf... he got all the girls' pictures on his wall."

Wendy is determined to defend her new boyfriend. "He's a ladies man... he knows what we want!" "Wendy!" Amber screams. "He's not a ladies man... he's a girl's boy; please Wendy, get real... He's barely 16... like you and I.... And why are you trying so hard to get his attention. If he doesn't notice you, keep it moving... you're better than that... way better!"

Wendy objects again, "But this is the thing, Amber; he does notice me. I think I'm the one. I'm telling you. That man..." She sees Amber's side-eye glance and corrects herself. "I mean that boy — uh ... that man..."

Seeing that she has her friend in a pickle, Amber begins to tease her. "Which is it, Wendy? You make me want to shake my head. He got you so confused…"

Wendy becomes very frustrated and she strongly objects, determined to hold on to the idea that she has a boyfriend. "No, Amber. You got me confused." She smiles to herself and says, "He got me …. captivated." She then picks up her phone and begins to kiss the pictures on Joey Carter's Facebook page.

Amber is determined to not let Wendy win this debate.

"Girl, if he's giving you any attention, it's because you're a tool he can use to make himself look good… you know, the more girls interested, the more desirable he will look to them all… please, don't be fooled. You need to see yourself… this is how you look…" Amber playfully snatches Wendy's phone out of her hand and begins to gaze into it, determining to conjure up her best impersonation of her best friend's puppy love. She begins to talk to Joey Carter as if she were Wendy.

Meanwhile, a beautifully dressed Bethany steps into the room unnoticed by the teenagers and begins to listen. Amber proceeds to talk to Joey with a sincere crush-voice. "Oh, Joey Carter, you all that and a bag of chips. An athlete's body indeed... and you can have me — all of me. As a sign of my commitment to you, I'm even willing to post crazy selfies of myself on your wall. I don't mind if the whole world sees just how crazy I am about you. You so fine, I will do anything for you... and I do mean anything. I'm ready for you to be my first. Oh Joey, I love you so much."

She begins to kiss the phone in the same comical manner that Wendy has been doing and then, she puts the phone back up to her ear as if she's talking to him. "I'm hoping you will be my last... I'm ready..." Bethany is about ready to intervene on Amber's open display of affection, but before she can make herself known, the doorbell's chimes change her mind. Amber, who doesn't know Bethany has been watching starts towards the door, but Bethany motions for her to move out of her way. "I got it," she snarls as she gives her daughter a quick look of dissatisfaction; Amber is confused.

Bethany opens the door and in struts Sandy Leach in a good mood, singing "Ladies Night" by Cool and the Gang. She struts around the living room modeling her extremely tight pants and her newly purchased Louis Vuitton handbag, half dancing to the song she is singing. "Oh yes, it's ladies' night and the feeling's right. Oh yes, it's ladies' night. Oh, what a night; oh, what a night!" She makes her voice go down to an extremely low pitch and humorously wiggles her body. Then continues the song in a different pitch. "Oh yes, it's ladies' night and the feeling's right. Oh yes, it's ladies' night — at Chaney's bar."

She lets out a hearty laugh and then greets everyone. "How y'all doing tonight? Hello Amber — Wendy..." Bethany greets her friend with an insincere compliment on her wardrobe. "Sandy, them pants are talking." Not catching the insincerity, Sandy proudly agrees with her friend. "Yep, sure to get some man's attention tonight ... and if they don't work...." She holds up her Louis Vuitton bag as if it were a prized possession, "... this will! Woot... Louis Vuitton, baby... how you like, Bethany?"

Hoping to impress her friend, she says, "You know this is their signature bag for the season." Bethany tells the truth about the bag to her friend, but points out an interesting fact about her character. "It's beautiful, Sandy; but how were you able to get that?" She lowers her voice so the girls don't hear. "You know that's a mortgage payment; right?!" Sandy naively responds, "Oh, you know I know how to finagle some things around to get what I want." She refuses to acknowledge what Bethany is insinuating and tries to offer a valid reason to splurge on herself. "This is my gift to myself for the year... sort of an early Christmas."

Realizing her banter is not working with Bethany, she insists on dropping the subject. "Now, come on with all this idle talk; we got business to take care of... Chaney's Ladies Night. You know we got to get there before eight unless you paying our cover charge tonight." She stops, playfully bats her eyes and asks Bethany, "By the way, you got my first drink; right?"

Bethany ignores Sandy's question, after all, every Thursday night, she pays for all the drinks. Sandy feels the need to ask because she just got called out concerning how she spends her mortgage money. Bethany blows it off because, while it looks like Sandy gets over on her, Bethany always knows just how far she will let her friend use her. Changing the subject, Sandy says, "I'm ready. You driving, or am I?"

Sandy strikes a pose perfectly displaying her fitted pants and expensive handbag. "Now, you know we got to floss the Mercedes..." Without saying a word, Bethany grabs her keys off the wall by the door and says, "Let's go!" Sandy resumes the song she was singing earlier as she strikes another perfect pose to tease the teenagers watching her. "If you hear any noise ... it's me and the boys; its ladies' night..."

Bethany stops and looks at Sandy. "Sandy ..." says Bethany, "... you know that's not the lyrics, right?! If you hear any noise, it's me and the boys? Girl, it's — if you hear any noise, it isn't the boys; its ladies' night." Sandy beams with pride before answering her friend. She says, "I know; this my version though." They both laugh and Bethany joins in singing the chorus with her friend. "Oh yes, it's ladies' night and the feeling's right. Oh yes, it's ladies' night; oh, what a night ... oh what a night! Oh yes, it's ladies' night and the feeling's right. Oh yes, it's ladies' night; oh, what a night." They sing all the way out the door. Bethany motions a boisterous farewell to Amber and Wendy as she disappears out of the front door.

After the door closes, Amber speaks first. "Let me see... Wendy, at the rate you're going, you are Sandy in about ten years." They both laugh as Amber continues. "Promise me you won't grow up to be like Sandy." Wendy playfully answers her friend. "Okay, but those pants were cute... you think they could fit me?" Amber snaps, "Wendy! What you going to do with those floozy mamma pants? Even Joey Carter wouldn't be impressed..."

Wendy gets invigorated at the thought of Joey Carter. "Speaking of... let's get back to the matter at hand: Joey..." Amber cuts her off before she can get his full name out of her mouth, refusing to give any more of her precious time to him.
"You know what, Wendy? I'm done talking about Joey Carter for the day. If you want to spend your

waking hours daydreaming about a boy who has no power to make your future bright, go right ahead... Besides, you're better than that. You got it going on, Wendy."

Wendy beams with a smile, "I know; right? I'm an honor student, I'm funny and creative... likable, and I have my own personal style."

Amber agrees. "Right ... if he can't appreciate those qualities about you from a distance or want to get to know you, he doesn't deserve to be all up in your personal space... cause if he in your personal space, he in mine too... I'll mess around and crack him upside the head."

They both laugh and Amber pulls an envelope out of her backpack. "Meanwhile, look what college I was invited to attend for winter break." Wendy snatches the letter and proceeds to peruse it aloud. "Dear Ms. Amber Clearwater, Congratulations, you are invited to attend our Medical Research pre-college program...here in beautiful Durham, North Carolina... Duke University... Amber ... Congratulations."

Amber gives her friend a serious look as she broaches a subject that is dear to her. "Wendy, have you started thinking about what colleges you're going to apply to yet? Wendy nonchalantly answers with, "No, I ..." Amber cuts her friend off and prepares to go off on her. "Why not, Wendy?" Amber waits a few seconds and then proceeds to answer her own question.

"I'll tell you why... You are distracted, and that is the devil's plan. If he can keep us focused on boys, how many hairstyles we can wear within a month's time, what cliques and clubs we are invited to join based on our looks, popularity or our parents' income, then he can prevent us from achieving our highest potential. He can tear our self-esteem down and cause us to feel rejected, useless and hopeless. When we start feeling like that... we are likely to become pregnant before the age of 17 and less likely to graduate high school. The devil wants us to become so depressed that we begin to abuse alcohol and drugs. Did you know that one out of six kids our age is likely to commit suicide and one out of twelve actually do try?"

Wendy is in awe of her friend's wisdom, "Amber, you so wise. Those are wise words... Where you learn all that?" Amber responds by eagerly seizing the opportunity for an evangelistic moment. "In youth group at my church. My pastors are real. They be talking about everything in life... sex, purity, getting good grades ..." Amber takes a moment to roll her eyes to the back of her head, suggesting that what she's about to say really hits home with her. She finishes the list with, "... and honoring our parents, even when they don't deserve it."

Without thinking about what she is actually saying, Wendy blurts out, "Oh, maybe I should go with you more often." She quickly realizes what she has just committed to and tries to change her tune. "I was just playing." Of course, Amber seizes the moment and counters with, "Matter of fact, Mamma gave me more than enough money for our upcoming Youth Explosion Conference next weekend, so I took the liberty of registering you as well."

She smiles at her friend before sealing the deal. "You can be my guest." Wendy whines because she knows there is no way out of this one. "Aw man, Amber ...now you know I don't do well with so much Jesus... All weekend?" Amber endearingly pats her friend on the back as she reassures her, "You'll be alright."

Wendy snaps out of her whiny voice and changes the subject. "Oh, by the way; how is David Jr.? I sure do miss him around here." The mood changes for the girls, and Amber answers her friend. "He's getting better. I'm praying he will be home and well by Thanksgiving..." Wendy looks at the calendar and realizes that Thanksgiving is just a month away as Amber continues to update her friend on her brother's condition.

"Yes, the doctors have been trying out different medications to see what will work and they want to keep him under observation as well... but Wendy, there is coming a day when he won't have to take medication because I know God hears my prayers." Determined to encourage Amber, Wendy makes a commitment to be there for her best friend. "Well then, I guess I better go to this Youth Conference with you so I can learn how to help you pray some mighty prayers... for our brother."

They look at one another and smile, and then, Wendy gets an afterthought. "Ah, but can we go shopping this weekend for some clothes for this conference? I want to get me some of Sandy Leach's 'it's me and the boys' floozy mamma pants." Amber leans in and hugs her friend. "You need Jesus," she says as she gives her another hug and they both burst into infectious laughter.

Chapter Eight

SEX TALK VS. COLLEGE TALK

Early the next morning, Bethany enters the kitchen, adjusting her clothes as she finishes getting dressed. She begins to go through her morning ritual of vitamin taking and coffee making, but she gets a little dizzy. She takes a seat at the kitchen table to recover. Moments later, Roy, Bethany's take home date from last night, enters the kitchen from Bethany's bedroom. He looks like he can be John Travolta's stand-in double in the movie Saturday Night Fever. He is fully dressed in black leather bell bottom pants, a waist length black leather jacket and a red polyester wide collar button down shirt. "I can almost hear the Bee Gees singing Night Fever," Bethany thinks to herself as Roy enters the kitchen.

As he approaches Bethany at the table, he speaks, "So, what are we having for breakfast, Mommy?"

His thick Spanish accent breaks the illusion that he is the actual character, Tony Manero, in the Movie 'Saturday Night Fever'. His child-like energy places his age range at no more than twenty years old. "Mommy, let's have some bacon and eggs and some pancakes this morning. I have a big appetite this morning from such an energized night."
He moves his hips from side to side. "Mommy, you had me working overtime." Bethany can hardly understand what he is saying because of his thick accent, however, at the mention of food, she becomes nauseated. "Ah, I really don't have time for a big breakfast this morning ... uh... it's Roy; right?"

Roy doesn't miss a beat and changes the subject as he begins to explore the surroundings. "So, Mommy, what do you do for a living?" As he looks around the house, he's obviously impressed and answers his own question, "... this is a nice living." Bethany tries to find an opportunity to get rid of her one-night-stand.

"Yeah, so here's the thing, Roy. I hadn't planned on doing breakfast with you so..." Before she can finish, Amber, dressed in her robe, comes into the kitchen and begins to prepare a bowl of cereal. She greets the couple with a short, "Good morning" before taking her seat. Bethany notices that Amber is not dressed for school and begins to scold her daughter.

"Amber, what are you doing? You're not even dressed..." Just then Roy cuts her off with awkward, immature humor. "Oh okay, Mommy. I get it. It's a family affair. Breakfast for three..." He turns to flirt with Amber and says, "Hello there. You're pretty..." Bethany finishes her statement to Amber, and in the same breath, addresses Roy, "You're going to be late for school! Roy, I told you, no breakfast!"

Without looking up from her cereal bowl, Amber says to her mother, "It's Teacher Work Day; there is no school today." Roy refuses to let go of the idea of breakfast and again shows his immaturity. He continues his playful banter with, "Oh, no school. It's okay Mommy; my treat. I'll take the both of you out for breakfast..."

Bethany is finally fed up with Roy's persistence. She stands to her feet and loudly rebukes him. "Roy, will you stop already?! I said nooooo breakfast... and stop calling me Mommy!" Roy quickly responds to Bethany as he watches Amber with lustful eyes. He says, "Well, you really could be my mommy. I'm just eighteen." Bethany is appalled. "What?! You told me that you were..." Bethany starts towards him. "You know what?! Never mind... just ..." She nudges him by the shoulders with both hands to escort him to the door. "It's time to go." She pushes him out and hastily shuts the door in his face. Without missing a beat, she turns her attention to her daughter.

"So, a teacher work day, huh? Good, I want to talk to you about something anyway. She gestures for Amber to make her way to the sofa. "Come ... have a seat with me for a moment." Amber finishes her bowl of cereal and joins her mother on the sofa. Bethany's mood suddenly changes. "Look at my daughter; you are all grown up... so fast, right before my eyes... and I've recently come to realize that we have not had that talk... you know ... about, you know... boys and... you. Now, I know it's overdue, but I hope I'm not too late..."

Amber has a confused look on her face. "Mom, what are you talking about?" Bethany's mood slightly shifts back to serious. "Amber, I'm trying to have a conversation with you about sex." With the same confused look, Amber answers, "Okay...???"

Bethany softens her mood again and continues with, "Of course, I would have hoped that you would wait until you're married." Amber, finally catching on to where the conversation is headed and begins to object. "Mom, that won't ..." Determined to have the birds and the bees conversation with her daughter, Bethany cuts Amber off and continues, "However, I know that kids today are a lot more sophisticated than the kids in my generation ... so... I'm taking you to my gynecologist next week to get you set up for birth control. Until then, I have some condoms to give you."

She reaches in her handbag, pulls out a few packs of condoms and shoves them in Amber's hand. "Please, be safe if you are going to..." Amber cuts her mother off and says, "Are you serious? Really!" Offended and embarrassed, she tries to give the condoms back to her mother. "I don't need those ... I'm not having sex."

Bethany refuses to take the condoms and tries to shove them back to Amber. She counters, "Amber, you don't have to pretend with me. I overheard your conversation last night. It's okay." She tries to take a sincere moment with her daughter. "I just hope that the boy would mean something to you..." By this time, Amber becomes enraged at her mother's assumption and throws the condoms across the room. "You are serious... You don't know me at all! I'm nothing like you! You heard what you wanted to hear last night."

She stands to her feet, hoping to get away from her mother and far away from this conversation. She continues, "You want me to be like you so you don't look so bad bringing your weekly dose of men home..." Bethany interjects, "Excuse me?" But before she can get anything more out of her mouth, Amber allows her pinned up opinion of her mother to spill out of her mouth. "Please, Mom! That boy who just left could have been my boyfriend... I'm just saying..."

Bethany is taken aback by her daughter's honesty. "Now, Amber..." But Amber cuts her off again, and while managing to put a few feet in distance between herself and her mother, she continues with the raw truth. "I'm nothing like you. I happen to believe that sex is sacred and marriage is sacred. I took a pledge of purity with the teenagers at my church..." Bethany takes on an argumentative tone with her daughter, "Purity?! Right! Let's see how long that lasts. Please! I was young once. Before the year's end, you could be asking me for money for an abortion."

Amber stops in her steps, takes a moment to calm down and changes her tone with her mother. "You don't get it; do you? Mom, I try so hard just so I don't end up like you... Miserable! I go to school, I get good grades, and I'm a good girl on purpose. I choose to honor God with my body and do it His way." By this time, tears are streaming down Amber's brave face. "You don't ever have to worry about me coming up pregnant... because I have a plan...and by God's grace, I will fulfill it..." Bethany refuses to be moved by her daughters tears and continues with the same argumentative spirit. "A plan?!" Amber snaps back to her mother and reaches into her school bag that happens to be laying on the floor. "Yes, a plan. I'm going to Duke University next year after graduation."

She pulls out papers and waves them in the air at her mom. "I have an opportunity to spend my winter break there and hopefully this summer as well. I've worked really hard on the application process with my guidance counselor... I've been researching colleges and my guidance counselor says that more than likely, I will win an academic scholarship." Amber looks at her mother with a disgusted look on her face as she continues, "And you want to sit down with me and talk about safe sex, but you haven't even asked me about college."

There is a moment of silence between the two, and then Amber continues. She says, "I'm a junior, Mother, and you haven't even thought it important enough to talk to me about college..." Bethany offers an excuse. "Amber, I can afford to send you to college. You have a pretty wealthy college fund... I've been saving for some time now..."

Amber interjects, "That's not the point!" Uncle Benjamin enters the room, but he is unnoticed by the two. Amber continues to yell at her mom with disbelief. "You are missing the whole point. But, why am I surprised? You're incapable of thinking about anyone else. Your mind is conditioned to put Bethany first. I've watched you for years...turn a cold heart... for a while, I couldn't understand why...I understand you lost your husband and had to work really hard... but when we lost our father, we lost our mother too."

"Amber!" Uncle Benjamin attempts to quiet Amber from her cruel attack on her mother, but to no avail. Amber has past the point of no return so, she continues. "You ignore your children... you can't even look at your son. It's easiest for you to throw money at us and withhold love and affection from us..."

Uncle Benjamin continues to try to silence the cruel truth coming out of Amber's mouth. "Now, that's enough young lady; have some respect!" Bethany takes a seat on the couch, holding her stomach as if she is going to be ill. Amber continues as if her uncle's command has fallen on deaf ears. "With you, it's how much money you can make and impress others with, and how many men you can bring home and then send away..."

Uncle Benjamin has heard enough and he raises his voice to silence his niece. "Amber! Quit!" In the same moment, Bethany leaps to her feet and crosses the room to her daughter. When she reaches Amber, she gives her a solid slap across her face. There is a long silence. Then with angry tears streaming down her face, Amber opens her mouth to speak just one more time.

"I try really hard to reach God and to know Him... because I see that you don't want God... but you are miserable...so I want Him all the more." She squares her shoulders off and says, "Yes, look at me, Mother, I am all grown up, right before your eyes, but I'm nothing like you... No thank you, I don't need that sex talk... I'm good..."

Without taking her eyes off her mother...." Amber backs away a few steps, and then turns her back on her mother. She then leaves the room, headed to her bedroom. Uncle Benjamin takes a step towards Bethany to console her. "Bethany, are you alright?" An embarrassed, angry and sick Bethany cannot bring herself to make eye contact with her brother-in-law. Instead, she starts toward her own bedroom. "I don't feel so well," she says. "I need to go lay down."

As he watches her leave the room, he notices the condoms on the floor and goes to pick them up, wondering what they are.
"Well, good morning, Benjamin." He didn't notice his mother's arrival until she spoke. "Where is everyone? You ready to drive me out to visit with David? Lord knows he could use the company." Still standing with the condoms in his hand, he answers his mother and says, "I thought you wanted to go out there tomorrow."
Mama Netty answers with enthusiasm, "Oh yes", she says. "I want to go tomorrow too. I thought I'd go today and tomorrow. I'll stay over here tonight, so we can get off to an early start."
"Yes, Mama Netty. I can drive you out there this morning." He submits to the plans as Mama Netty continues to ramble on.

"His mother acts like she's too busy to go out there to visit with him; she makes a big deal about being able to pay the bills though. I guess it's just as well. He tends to not do so well when her name is even mentioned."

"On second thought," Uncle Benjamin offers an alternative to his mother's plans. "Mama Netty, don't you think you can take a few days off?" He reassures her. "David will be okay if you don't visit him for a few days. Besides, there are some days you go there and you're not even able to see him." She quickly objects, "Faith has to be there no matter if we can visit with him or not! I'm going everyday if I can; Lord willing! I have to keep a good eye on my grandson. He's going to overcome this... I'll see to it... those doctors trying to give him mental disease." She looks at her son with dignity. "Our pastor prayed generational curses away from him. The devil is not going to take my grandson too!"

With that, Uncle Benjamin backs off and submits, once again, to his mother's wishes. "Well, alright then. I'm about ready... just give me a minute." Uncle Benjamin drops the condoms on the counter in front his mother and disappears into Amber's room. "Well hurry up now. I want to beat the traffic this morning..." She picks up one of the packages of condoms and says, "What are these... condoms? What is...? Oh, he's coming to church with me on this Sunday; no excuses... condoms?!"

Chapter Nine

A Catalyst for Change

It's early Saturday morning and Mama Netty is up singing and cooking in the kitchen. An annoyed Bethany interrupts and Mama Netty greets her. "Well good morning, Bethany; you up pretty early. Oh, that's right; this is Saturday. You're off to your exercising class." She looks up from what she is doing and right away sees that Bethany is not feeling well. "What's wrong with you? You have the flu?"

Bethany ignores her mother-in-law's inquiry about her health. "Mamma, can you keep it down out here? I need to sleep for just about another hour. I'm not going to that exercise class this morning." Mama Netty is in a good mood and answers Bethany, taking the opportunity to update her on the plans for the day. "Yeah, sure I can. I have to go on and get ready so that we can beat the traffic this morning. We are going to sit with David Jr. again on today. Would you like for me to tell him anything for you?" Without waiting for Bethany's response, she scurries off to the bedroom area.

Just then, the doorbell chimes ring out and Bethany makes her way to the door. A high-energy Sandy Leach, dressed in her workout gear, springs through the door. "Good morning, good morning and good morning. You ready to do this... face Boa. It's the last Saturday of the month... you know what that means... show time." She notices that Bethany is still in her robe. "Hey, how come you are not dressed? I know you don't want to be the reason for extra push-ups?" Realizing that something is wrong, Sandy questions Bethany. "You okay?" Bethany attempts to quickly get rid of her friend and responds, "Yes, I'll be okay. I'm sorry. Sandy, I forgot to call you to cancel for today. I'm not feeling up to any physical activity." She attempts to lead her friend to the door. "I need to go back to bed for a few more hours."

Sandy doesn't take Bethany's lead; instead, she invites herself to a cup of coffee and a sit-down with her friend. "Well, I'm here now; you might as well join me for a cup of coffee before I leave. I'm not going to boot-camp if you're not going... I only go to that class because you go." She makes her way to the freshly brewed coffee, "Anyway, come on; have a cup of coffee with me."

She prepares to pour two cups of coffee and Bethany responds, "Alright, I'll sit with you for a few minutes, but no coffee for me. I want to go back to bed." Sandy puts one cup back in the cupboard and begins to pour coffee in the other mug. "So, what's wrong? You got the flu? What are your symptoms...?" Bethany, tries to escape the conversation at hand. "No, I'm just a little tired... and..." Sandy cuts her off mid-sentence and continues. "Nauseated... sick at the stomach... dizzy and light headed."

Bethany understands that her secret is out and she gives in to the conversation that she's been trying to avoid.
"You make it sound so real. Yes, all the above... Sandy, what am I going to do?"

Without missing a beat, Sandy offers her opinion. "Girl, how old are you? You can't afford to have no more babies... especially because the two you have already are about to be grown."

Bethany responds, half listening to her friend. "I know; what am I going to do with a ... I can't even say the word..."

"Look," Sandy adds, "I know a good private doctor. What are you about three weeks or so?" She thinks for a moment, and then comes to her own conclusion. "You could be more... go ahead and deal with this as soon as possible...you have to get it behind you."

"I know," Bethany agrees, "I have to face the truth, but I just need a little time to rap my head around this..."

Sandy strongly objects to the idea of Bethany taking more time to act on this matter. "Time?! Just don't take too much time, Bethany. Trust me, you do not want to take your time on this. The longer you wait, the more complicated it gets..."

Bethany responds, "Well I don't plan on discussing this situation with any potential fathers...I plan on keeping the drama down... I don't need any drama..."

"Exactly! And why do you have to discuss it with anyone... including your family when you are planning on getting rid of the problem? ... I mean... really..." At this last statement from Sandy, Bethany is taken aback as to what her friend has been suggesting. "Wait; what?! Getting rid of the problem? Sandy, I'm not planning on 'getting rid of the problem.' The thought has not even crossed my mind." She takes a moment to think to herself. "Now, I will admit — this is a bit hard to swallow, but I'm not in a frame of mind to abort." She looks at her friend, horrified at her suggestion. "That doesn't even feel right..."

Sandy has the same callus attitude about the subject and attempts to talk some sense into Bethany. "Girl, have you lost your mind? A baby? What you going to do with a baby?" She looks at Bethany and waits for a response, but then continues, "You probably don't even know who the father is." Then, as if she has figured out her friend's motives, she accuses Bethany. "What? You're going to try to trap you a husband? Oh, I see; you are going to let Winston think it's his. Girl, I didn't know you had all that game. But I still say to you, you need to get rid of that problem."

"Excuse me!" Bethany has had enough of Sandy's insults and proceeds to shut her down. "First of all, I don't need a man to help me or my child; last I checked, my bills are paid and then some. Secondly, there aren't going to be any games here. If I'm grown enough to lay with a man, I'm grown enough to deal with the consequences. I might have some issues, but I'm not that low. Lastly, I have two almost grown children — as you pointed out. That would mean I'm grown... grown enough to make my own decisions about my life."

She stands to her feet and begins to move towards the door as she continues to speak. "Now, if you can't get with that, then as far as I'm concerned, the only problem I need to get rid of is you." She reaches the door, opens it and says, "I feel a headache coming on ... it's time for you to go." A humbled Sandy rises to her feet, makes her way to the door, and without saying a word or making eye contact with Bethany, leaves.

Bethany closes the door, adjusts the knot on her bathrobe belt and goes to take a seat on the couch. She sits for a moment in silence, and then, in a moment of vulnerability, she whispers a prayer. She says, "Oh, God... what am I doing here.... ugh... I could do a lot better — I know." She looks up towards heaven and says, "Lord, I need you. There, I said it; I need your help."

She sits in another long moment of silence, and then she begins to speak in the direction of her front door. "An abortion?! Really, Sandy?! You're some kinda friend!" She chuckles to herself as she places her hand on her belly and says, "No. There's been too much death around here.... a baby... hmm ... new life..."

Mama Netty, Uncle Benjamin and Amber go into the kitchen and begin to gather food and supplies for the day's outing. Mama Netty notices Bethany sitting alone on the couch. "Oh, Bethany; you still here? I thought you went back to bed. We are all headed out to visit with David Jr. for the day. We are bringing him his favorite foods... you know he'll be coming home on next week. The doctors have everything all figured out."

Bethany doesn't respond, so there is a moment of silence. Mama Netty speaks again, "Are you sure that you don't want me to give him a message from you?" Again, more silence. To everyone's surprise, Bethany says, "Tell him that I love him." Everyone looks at one another with approval, gathers their items and then leaves out of the front door. As she sits with herself and her unborn baby, she ponders her thoughts. "We're going to be alright," Bethany reassures herself. "David Jr., you're going to be alright."

Chapter Ten

THE TRUTH SETS YOU FREE

It's a week later and the time has finally arrived for David Jr. to come home. Savannah is sitting on the sofa drinking a dark-colored beverage out of a glass. She quickly checks to see if anyone is looking before pulling a pint-sized bottle of whiskey out of her handbag to refresh her drink. Just after completing her mission, Amber abruptly speaks from the kitchen. "You alright, Auntie; can I get you anything?"

A startled Savannah answers, "No, for the umpteenth time, niece. I have everything I need. When are they supposed to be here though? We have been waiting a while now. All I wanna do is see my nephew. I'm going to see how he is doing and get out of here before she-wolf gets home." Amber chuckles, "She-wolf?!" "Auntie, you so funny.

I just talked to Mama Netty and they should be here in a few. They got held up in heavy traffic earlier."

Amber comes to where her aunt is sitting in the living room to take advantage of a private moment between the two. "Auntie, can I talk to you?" She takes a seat next to where she is sitting on the couch. Before answering, Savannah moves her drink to the other side of herself so that Amber doesn't get a whiff of the alcohol. "Sure Amber; what's up?" Amber responds with an innocent look on her face. "You and my mom; what happened?" Right away, Savannah's demeanor changes. "Aww Amber, I can't take heavy right now. No!" She waves her arms in the air. "No heavy conversations... I just want to see my nephew and get on my happy way."

Amber has never asked her Aunt questions concerning her relationship with Bethany or their upbringing. In her mind, it's always been a subject that has been off limits to talk about. Perhaps that perspective has to do with the hot-blooded tension that has been boiling between the two as early as Amber can remember. Or maybe it's because even though she and her aunt have an amicable relationship, Amber wouldn't consider it a close one.

There are various reasons for this fact. For one, there have not been very many occasions for a close relationship to grow — no family reunions and no family outings. Aside from occasional family dinners, Amber rarely sees her aunt. Another possible reason could be that on the rare occasions that Savannah is permitted to come around the family, she has always shown up heavily impaired by drugs and alcohol. This fact always made it difficult for Amber to even approach Savannah for a meaningful conversation.

Lastly, aunt and niece don't have too much in common, but Amber has always felt the need to protect her aunt in some way. Probably because, though Savannah is a strong woman, her addictions, in Amber's eyes, made her weak. All these things play a role in why so many family secrets are never discussed.

But lately, Amber's perspective about family and life has been changing. "I know, Auntie, but I have just been thinking a lot... about our family... and I just wanna know what happened because my pastor was just preaching on forgiveness. He said that an unwillingness to forgive leads to bitterness and is the number one reason most families are so dysfunctional."

She looks at her aunt and asks, "Wouldn't you say that our family is dysfunctional?" Savannah picks up her drink and takes a sip before she responds to her niece. "Amber, you don't know what dysfunction is... you got it easy. Your mamma is she-wolf. Don't get me wrong, but trust me when I tell you this: your grandmother — me and your momma's mother — now, she was she-wolf, devil from hell."

At the thought of her deceased mother, Savannah throws caution to the wind, pulls out the pint of alcohol from her handbag and begins to refresh her drink again. Amber objects with a chuckle, "Auntie? Now, you know you are not supposed to be drinking in here..." Savannah quickly cuts Amber off to justify her actions. "I know, Amber, but if you want to hear the truth, then I need some truth potion."

She finishes topping off her drink and puts the empty bottle back into her handbag. "I need to shake off this here inhibition..." Amber lifts her brows and says, "My grandmother was that bad? That's why Mamma never talks about her?" Savannah takes a mouth full of her alcoholic drink, holds it in her mouth for a second before swallowing it and begins to speak. "She was selfish... miserable... hateful...with no conscience, but I don't think your mother remembers too much of the bad — like I do."

She looks at her niece with a look of distress on her face and asks, "You sure you wanna hear this?" This question is more about Savannah not wanting to travel down this rarely traveled road of memories. But, Amber shakes her head in affirmation as she settles to a comfortable position on the couch next to her auntie. "Well, I guess you're old enough."

She begins. "Your grandmother —Red — they called her that because she was high yellow... a beautiful woman... could have had any man and anything she wanted. She was smart too... to this day, I can't understand why she chose the men she did. Nasty men — and they came one after another — she never changed the type ... always the same... weed smoking, gutter talking, non-working — a real job that is... and sex driven. She settled for way less than her lot in life and because of her taste in men, we suffered.

Mamma was so busy chasing these men that she forgot she had daughters with no father to watch out for them. Half the time, she was just as high as the men in her life... and she was preoccupied with chasing after them to keep the women they were chasing at bay." Amber interjects, "But, where was your father?"

At this time, Bethany enters from the front door and neither of the two notice her. She quietly stands behind the island in the kitchen and begins to listen to their conversation. Savannah answers Amber's question. "You ever heard the term 'rolling stone?' She doesn't wait for a response from her niece; instead, she quotes a line from the popular song from the seventies by The Temptations.

"Spend most of his time chasin' women and drinkin'! Well, that was our father; he was a rolling stone. He laid his head in a different woman's bed just about every night. Mamma and him were married. They got married young because at sixteen, Mamma got pregnant with me and Daddy was twenty. They were married, but I don't ever recall him living in the same house with us. We would see him from time to time, but I don't ever recall an intimate moment between the two: a kiss, a hug... and yet, they had three more babies after me." From the look on Bethany's face, this is news to her. Savannah continues to speak. "They had a long stormy relationship..."

Amber cuts her off again and asks, "Wait. Three more children?" She counts on her fingers, but only gets to one finger. "Mamma and... where are the other two?" "They both died; the first — another girl — was born after me and before your mamma. She lived just three days. Our little brother lived a full month in an incubator... then he passed away. I overheard the nurses talking about how mamma should have loved him more, how she didn't even show any warmth to him... They said he died because he knew his mother didn't want him." Amber interrupts her aunt again to ask another question. "Well, how did my grandfather take it?" "Please, by this time, daddy had landed a prison sentence." Savannah rolls her eyes to the back of her head in deep thought, "I don't even think he knew Mamma had another baby... I could be wrong; we lost contact with him after that." Savannah seems to be thinking to herself at this point and says with sadness in her voice, "I think that's why Mamma became so bitter and cold." She looks at Amber and makes a half smile, "She really did love him. After all, he was her first love and only love, probably." She continues after a moment. "Every man after that was just out of convenience, I think."

She takes another sip of her drink and then continues, "This is when things really got dark for us. A single mother with two daughters... and an appetite for men of different sorts...." Savannah's demeanor changes and then, she stops as if she's finished reminiscing. Amber objects and begins to badger Savannah. "What do you mean? What happened?" When she sees that her aunt is not talking, she objects again. "Wait, you can't just stop, Auntie"

Savannah takes a deep breath and then exhales. She squirms on the sofa and then picks up her glass to chug down the remainder of her drink. After a moment, she takes another deep breath and slowly exhales. Afterwards, she reluctantly resumes her story. "Like I said, Mamma was self-absorbed... all she cared about was her next bottle of alcohol and the man-flavor of the month. I think she resented me being around — as if I was keeping her from her happy.

She didn't even notice when her man-flavor of the month started to notice me, but I remember... the first time... I had never seen a one hundred-dollar bill... I didn't even know such a thing existed. I was thirteen... and here I was faced with the option of being able to feel that crisp one hundred-dollar bill... to have it... all I had to do was ..."

Savannah abruptly stops again, realizing that she has never told her story before. Amber becomes impatient again. "Was what, Auntie? Was what?" A cloud of shame comes over Savannah as she realizes that she's getting ready to share with her innocent teenage niece graphic details of her childhood — a story that no one has ever heard. She decides to continue, but makes a mental note to edit out the shame.

"To this day, I can remember... it's as if my mind took a snapshot — this man with skin as black as the middle of the night. He had a vicious looking scar beginning from his right ear to clear across his forehead, to above his right eye." She closes her eyes as if doing so helps her to remember more vividly or perhaps shields her from the shame and she continues, "I remember the details of that scar as plain as day because he had a shiny bald head that made the scar look like something out of a horror movie. A big man — intimidating — not with words; he had very few."

She opens her eyes to check-in with her niece as she continues, "And that crisp one-hundred-dollar bill ... the way he held it ... It's a shame, she had no questions for her ten-year-old daughter who had just given her a crisp one hundred-dollar bill." She closes her eyes in order to think to herself for a moment. Then her eyes spring open as she remembers her mother's reaction. She stares at her niece with piercing eyes and then speaks again.

"You know, I once had a cat... it used to bring me dead birds and lizards and lay them at the front door as a gift." She looks at Amber and smiles as she explains the analogy. "They say that cats often do that out of instinct. It's in their nature to bring gifts. No one knows why. The experts think it's their way of saying thank you for feeding and taking care of them. They go out and hunt for prey and kill to feed you in the same way that mother cats feed their young. Isn't that something?

They are instinctual, or some feel that pet cats feel that they are responsible for their owners and they go out to hunt and bring the prey out of duty to take care of their owners. They say that you shouldn't react in a bad way when your pet cat brings you their prey as a gift. They are not acting bad; that's

just the way they know how to please you and to
say thank you for taking care of them." She looks
past Amber as she reasons with herself, "I wonder if
that's why Mamma reacted the way she did."

Amber begins to say something, but her mother
cuts her off. "Now, that's enough, Savannah... filling
this girl with all your lies... you know that never
happened. You live in fantasy-land. Mamma would
have never..." Savannah defensively snaps back at
Bethany, "How would you know, Bethany? You
were just three or four years old. You didn't have it
like I had it." She deliberately looks at Bethany to
make sure she hears what she has to say next. "I
made sure of that, not Mamma! Trust me, she was
not thinking about you."

Bethany snaps back at her sister. "Oh, and you
were?! Please, Savannah! The way I remember it —
you just described yourself and not Mamma..."
Savannah takes offense to her sister's ignorance
and snaps back at her. "What would you know? By
the time you were old enough to know anything,
Mamma was dead and buried in the ground... and I
was glad..."

At this point, Bethany leaves where she has been standing in the kitchen to go and confront her sister. "Glad that your own mother was dead?! What kind of a daughter..." Amber stands in front of Bethany to serve as a barrier between the two women. Savannah continues, ignoring her sister's insults. "She was miserable and she made everything living and breathing miserable, and I told myself that when I buried her, I buried misery in the same grave..."

Bethany's voice shakes as she continues to accuse her sister. "You wouldn't even talk about her or tell me about her! Now, you have a lot to say to my daughter..." Savannah has an answer for every accusation. "You didn't want to hear the truth..." Bethany is enraged at her sister and partly out of frustration, she yells at her, "I had a right to know..."

Just then, Mama Netty, Uncle Benjamin and David Jr. enter through the front door. Savannah sees them enter, but refuses to allow Bethany to win this debate. "To know what, Bethany? You had a right to know what?! That your mother was a drunk?"

Bethany vehemently defends her dead mother. "She wasn't the drunk. You were the drunk and still are!" With this, Bethany points her finger towards the door and motions to her sister with the other hand, "Get out my house you drunk…"

Mama Netty attempts to break up the shouting match by letting her presence be made known. "Hey, what's going on here… you two at it again?" Both sisters are oblivious to anyone else in the room as they continue to go back and forth with one another. "She was a whore, Bethany… Your mother was a miserable, drunk whore… a prostitute… and…"

Mama Netty goes to move Amber out of harm's way and takes up position between the ladies with her hands raised. She raises her voice above each of the sisters and shouts, "Not today! There has to be peace today!" She quickly turns her head to take a quick glance at her grandson. Bethany ignores Mama Netty's pleas and overrides her mother-in-law's commands with a louder voice.

"Now, you a lie! How low will you go, Savannah?!" Savannah continues, determining to get the full truth out for Bethany and the family to hear once and for all. She moves to the middle of the room and takes a stance much like a prostitute would do on a street corner. "When she died, I took over the family business… I guess that's how low I will go, Bethany!" By this time, she is standing alone in the middle of the living room floor. There is silence as the rest of the family stares at her.

Savannah pleads with her sister in a softer tone of voice this time, "… I did it for you, Bethany — for you…" Bethany rejects the idea of her sister being noble. "You did it for me? When have you ever done anything for anyone… you're a drunk and a druggie… everyone knows drunks and druggies are selfish people."

Amber has had enough of her mother's cruelty and attempts to calm her down. "Mamma, stop… can't you be nice for once?" Savannah agrees with Bethany's accusations, but she addresses Amber when she speaks. "She's right about the drugs. I won't lie; I needed the drink and the harder stuff …

to help me." Mama Netty comes to Savannah's rescue and says, "But you could get help now; it's not too late for you to turn things around. God is able."

Savannah continues to purge herself. She suddenly realizes that it's not help from the family that she's after; it's rescuing her sister. She pulls herself together and in a calm voice, she speaks to her sister. "Bethany, you were such a little thing — so beautiful and innocent." Tears begin to stream down her face as she remembers the innocence of her little sister.

"You knew what happiness was because you didn't see what I saw... I made sure of that. I wanted to make sure you had a good life. If I couldn't have happy, then I was going to make sure someone I cared about could. I wasn't going to be like Mamma. She was miserable... she wanted company in misery and so she chose me. I gave her what she wanted... and those men... I laid my gift out before her... but you, I needed to hold on to your innocence."

Bethany continues to refuse to accept the truth. "You're a liar... my Mamma was..." Savannah again offers the truth to Bethany as she finishes her sister's statement. "A whore..." Uncle Benjamin takes center stage with authority as he tries to get the ladies to calm down. "Okay now, that's enough — both of you!" He turns to Savannah and speaks to her directly. "Savannah, that's enough. Now, calm down and we can get you some help."

David Jr. speaks up in a rational tone for the first time in a long time. "No, Uncle Benny... Aunt Savannah needs to say these things. It's the truth that makes you free... Mamma needs the truth." Surprised, Bethany attempts to correct her son. "David, I'm glad you're home, but you need to stay out of this. I know the truth."

Savannah continues to unearth her truth to Bethany. "I was glad when she died. I knew in a few short years that she would choose you too... I was glad... my baby sister was going to be something in life. She was going to make it... it was too late for me, but for you?"

Bethany snaps back to her sister, refusing to acknowledge the danger her sister tells her that she was in. "Is that your excuse... you gave up in life because Mamma died?" But Savannah refuses to back down until she says all that needs to be said. She continues, "When she died, I had to make sure you stayed in school and had what you needed... it worked for a while, but when they started noticing my baby sister...and the drug had a hold of me..."

She takes a moment to reflect and then pleads with Bethany. "I tried to make it on minimum wage... but by that time, the drug was a monkey on my back ... I couldn't shake it ... I couldn't hold it together..." She looks at her sister with caring eyes and says, "I knew that I took you as far as I could take you and I just couldn't anymore."

Savannah's tears begin to stream down her face again. Bethany has heard the truth and the truth hurt. She begins to sob as she says to her sister what she's been wanting to say for a very long time. "So, you just threw me away... the one person I had in my life... and you just threw me away."

With a softer, more compassionate voice, Savannah attempts to comfort her sister. She says, "Bethany, it was just for a few years — you were in foster care, but you made it... when I had heard you graduated college... I said, we made it... we made it... my baby sister made something of herself... I celebrated... I pulled out my bottle and I had a drink for you."

Bethany finally gives up, but still not willing to acknowledge that she has heard the truth, she makes her announcement for all her family to hear. With coldness in her voice, she says, "I'm tired; I need to go lay down." She addresses Savannah once again and says, "Savannah, you can stay to visit with your nephew, but when I get up, I expect you to be gone." She callously turns her back and starts to leave, but Savannah has one more thing to say. Something about the sound in her voice causes Bethany to stand still with her back turned from her sister.

"You used to have me put Band-aids on the neighborhood children." She sees that she has her sister's attention and proceeds to remind her of who she used to be. "Any one of them get a scrape or a bruise, you'd bring them to the house for a band-aid... because you couldn't stand to see anyone hurting. I remember that little girl that lived across the way; she was a few years younger than you. Bonnie, was her name, I think. Her mother passed away and in the middle of the night, you brought her back to our house, sat with her hand in your hand and because she cried, you cried."

Tears continue to stream down her face as she continues. "Nobody had to tell you to care or do good; it was just in you. You were something special. She wipes the tears from her eyes and tries to dry her face with her sleeve. "After I let you go, when I was out there in my worst state, all I had to do was think about you and I felt better... because you were the one thing I did right. But, what happened to you, Bethany? It's funny — how hard I tried to shield you from Mamma, but you're just like her... and the thing is... you didn't even know her that well..."

A lone tear rolls down one of Bethany's cheeks, but none of the family sees it. She appears to remain unmoved by her sister's words. "You heard me, Savannah. Don't be here when I get up from my nap." Bethany resumes to make her way to her room while the others begin to console one another. David Jr. gives Savannah a big loving hug.

Chapter Eleven

GIVE THE DEVIL A BLACK EYE, KICK HIM WHERE IT HURTS!

The doorbells chime rings out into the silence and a few moments later, Amber emerges from down the hallway to answer the door. A distraught Wendy steps in and begins to harass her friend. "What took you so long to answer the door, Amber?" Amber replies objectively, "What do you mean? It only rang once, Wendy! What's going on? What's the urgency?"

As Wendy makes a bee-line to the sofa and plops down, Amber follows her. She notices the big bruise and the bloody lip on her friend's face. "Wendy! What happened to you? What happened to your face? Let me get Mama Netty..." She reaches for her cell phone and says to Wendy, "We need to get you to the hospital."

Wendy becomes panicky and shouts, "No! Don't get Mama Netty. I don't want her to know... be quiet... is she here? Is anyone here?" Amber stands, holding her cell phone looking at her friend with a puzzled look on her face. "No, nobody is here, but let me call Netty!" She starts to make the call from her cell phone again, but Wendy becomes even more agitated and snatches the phone from Amber. "No, Amber! I don't want you to call her. I don't need a hospital."

Amber sits next to Wendy on the couch. "Okay. Calm down." With that, Wendy replies, "I am calm down; you calm down." Amber snaps back at her friend, "I am calm; you calm down." Wendy shoots back, "I am calm..." Amber finally shouts at her friend, "Wendy! What happened?!" Wendy responds with another,"Calm down," and then she takes a moment to gather her composure. She looks at her friend with embarrassed eyes. "You were right, Amber. You were right about him. He is just a playa." Amber looks at her friend and with panic in her voice, she asks, "Is this about Joey Carter? What did he do to you?"

Wendy looks down at the floor in shame as she confesses her fault to her friend. "I'm so embarrassed... I'm such a fool. Who was I kidding?" Amber impatiently cuts her friend short to get to the bottom line. "But what happened? Wendy ... Did he, you know... did he ..." Wendy pulls out her cell phone and scrolls to a message. "He texted me just before school let out today."

She reads the message with the same embarrassment in her voice. "Bae, you are looking fresh today. We are getting ready to bounce this thing to the next level... straight up, see you at my crib with the quickness... keep dis on the down low though." Amber interjects, "Wendy, tell me you didn't go to his house?" The look on Wendy's face makes it clear to Amber that indeed, she went to his house. "Alone?!" Amber appears to be both sympathetic for her friend and furious. "I don't know what I was thinking."

She begins to share the details. "When I got there, everything was fine at first. He was real nice to me — a real gentleman. We were sitting in his front room talking. Then, he handed me a soda and told me to drink it down... and he got up and left for a minute. When he came back, his shirt was off and he said — did I want to prove to him that I was into him, and that he wanted me to do him a favor."

Amber has a look of horror on her face as she attempts to get a better understanding of what happened to her friend. "A favor?! This doesn't sound good...you didn't drink that drink; did you?"

Wendy continues with the same embarrassed look on her face, picking the story up where she left off. "Before I could even answer, he took me by my hand and led me to a room in the back of his house. She gets a little teary eyed and she looks at her friend. "Amber, when I walked in, there were about three or four other guys there — at least two I had never seen before. There were bottles of alcohol and the smell of weed and the music was kinda loud. I didn't know what I was doing there...I didn't know what to do. Then Joey asked me to take off my blouse because they wanted to take a picture with me."

Amber puts her hand on Wendy's shoulder and, in the most compassionate voice she can muster up, she begins to console her friend. "Wendy, I'm so sorry for you..." Wendy looks up from the floor at her friend and with her brows furrowed up, speaks to her friend with a little attitude in her voice. "Don't feel sorry for me; feel sorry for him. All I knew was that I had to get up outta there."

Wendy stops for a moment, changes her voice and says, "Amber, but something happened to me though. You remember what your pastor kept telling us to say to our neighbor at the Youth Conference?" Amber, wondering what this has to do with anything, decides to play along with her friend, and they both chant the line together, "Turn to your neighbor and say, you got to give the devil a black eye. Hit him where it hurts."

Amber, stealing the opportunity to be the evangelist that she is, begins to recount the entire message. "Then, he would say, 'Seize the moment to win the victory.' Yes, as many times as he had us repeat that... when he was teaching us about spiritual warfare and how to battle the enemy with spiritual weapons... like prayer, fasting... obedience to God."

Wendy cuts her friend short. "Amber, Amber, Amber...I don't know bout no spiritual weapons. All I know is that Joey Carter started walking towards me and everything blacked out for a moment. I could hear this voice as clear as day say to me, "Give the devil a black eye; hit him where it hurts." I couldn't hear nothing, see nothing... All I know is — I got into my best crouching tiger, hidden dragon position. It felt like slow motion ..."

She rises from her seat on the couch and stands in front of her friend. She reenacts her best Karate position with one knee up and her hands raised above her head as she struggles to balance herself on one foot. She continues, "... and I gave the devil a black eye." She motions punching him in the face. "And I hit him where it hurts." She motions kicking him in his groin. "I seized the moment to win the victory... I got up on out of there."

Amber's mouth drops open as she is amazed at her friends' exploits, "What?!" She thinks for a moment and asks, "Well, how did you get a busted lip?" Wendy thinks back for a moment and says, "You know; I really don't know." She then comes up with a possible scenario. "It could have been when I was getting up out of there. I actually looked like I was part of the football team." She and Amber begin to laugh. "I think I plowed over at least two of those guys that were standing in front of me. I didn't have time to say excuse me, if you know what I mean."

They both laugh harder and share a sigh of relief. Then Wendy takes a serious moment. "Amber, God is real." She begins to explain what she means with a reverential attitude. "When Joey gave me that drink and told me to drink it down, and when he went into the other room, I heard this voice say to me, "You are not a fool; do not drink that." Amber breaks in to hasten the answer. "But did you drink it?" Wendy shakes her head. "No," she says. "I watered his mother's plant with it." She bursts into laughter, but quickly catches herself and becomes seriously reverential again. "I was more afraid of disobeying the voice. Somehow I knew it was God."

She looks at her friend with the same serious tone to get her point across. "I can't explain this, but something came over me when I stood up to them. It wasn't me, but it was me. All I have to say is God is real." Amber chimes in in agreement with her friend and says, "Yes, He is and He is good all the time! I'm just glad you're okay. You do understand that this could have been really bad, Wendy; right!?" Wendy drops her head again in shame and answers her friend, "Yeah, I know... I'm so embarrassed. I was just fooling myself that someone like Joey Carter could be genuinely interested in me."

She looks at Amber with panic when she thinks about encountering Joey Carter and the other boys at school. "How am I going to face him now?" Amber answers her friend with pride and shock in her voice. "What?! Wendy, listen to you? Do you realize what you're saying and what just happened to you? Joey Carter is a knuckle head." She quotes her friend, "Someone like him ... please! He obviously has a whole lot of issues if he has to treat girls like that. He doesn't think very much of himself if he has to drug girls to get them to sleep with him."

She looks at her friend with a big smile on her face and says, "But God thinks a whole lot about you because He did not permit Joey Carter or those boys to do to you what they probably have done to others. Please, I feel sorry for him. You know what I'm thinking about now? How is Joey Carter going to be able to face seeing you at school for the rest of the school year?" She recreates Wendy's crouching tiger; hidden dragon pose and they both begin to laugh. "Thank you for being here for me, friend. What would I do without you? Just for the record... I was kinda paying attention at the conference; thanks for inviting me."

Amber looks mischievously as she begins to harass Wendy about Bible study night. "Oh, so does this mean you're going to stop giving me the run around on Friday nights for youth meeting?" Wendy answers, "Well, let's just say this — I know I need Jesus." She throws her hands up to the air and says, "He's going to have to do the rest...cause the Lord knows I'm a mess." They both laugh as Amber agrees with her friend.

Wendy changes the subject, and with another serious look on her face, she says, "Oh, yeah; but guess what I did do? I have begun the college search and I, my friend, have applied for ... drum roll, please.... Duke University. Mrs. Rose, our counselor, says with my grade point average, her letter of recommendation and a good application essay, I could win a scholarship from the college of my choice. I've already gotten plenty of letters from colleges inviting me to apply."

Amber is beside herself with joy for her friend. "This is great news! I'm glad to see that my old friend is back on her game." They high-five and fist-bump one another and Wendy says, "Yeah, I really was paying attention to you; I've been doing some soul-searching, especially since the conference. I mean it, Amber. The conference changed my life... and what I just escaped today? Oh, I think I will be on the right track for a while though." Amber sings to her friend in a silly voice, "Amen, Amen, Amen!"

Just then, Mama Netty, Uncle Benjamin and David Jr. burst through the front door. All three are focused on their conversation. "Mama Netty, I'm telling you, I feel just fine... I'm not crazy," David exclaims to his grandmother. "I know David, and I am glad to hear you say it, but I don't think you should stop taking your medicine just yet. Don't get me wrong. I know you are healed. God answers prayers. You are free from any generational curses or sickness in the name of Jesus! However, those doctors had you taking some strong medication while you were getting treatment." Uncle Benjamin reassures his nephew as well. "David, I agree with your grandmother. Let's just wean your system the correct way — the safe way. All she is saying is we must use wisdom here... no footholds for the devil."

David notices his sister and Wendy sitting on the sofa, and without responding to his two elders, he goes to greet the two on the couch. He gives Amber a hug and greets Wendy at the same time.
"Hello Wendy."
"Hi David Jr. Good to have you home. You know we been missing you around here. When are you coming back to school?"

He glances at his grandmother and answers, "Soon, I guess…. what happened to your lip?" Wendy lowers her voice so as not to draw attention to herself, "Oh, nothing… I, um, bit it… it will be okay." But it's too late because Mama Netty is already standing over Wendy to examine the busted lip. "Oh, that is a nasty cut."

She starts towards the medicine cabinet, interrogating Wendy as she goes. "Tell me how you got this cut again? Will you be staying for dinner? You know you are always welcome." Wendy rises to her feet, quickly gathers her things and moves toward the door to make a quick exit. "No thank you, Mama Netty. Matter of fact, I was just leaving. Mama is looking for me to come home for dinner. Nice to see you all again. David Jr, you know I love you… talk to you later, Amber."

Wendy disappears through the door. "Well now that was pretty peculiar… you know that girl lives here. As long as I've known her, she has never turned down dinner." Mama Netty gives Amber an inquisitive look and asks, "Amber, is everything okay?" Amber quickly answers, "Yes, Ma Netty; all is well, now."

She switches her attention to her little brother. "So, what's this about your medication, David?" He answers his sister with a nonchalant attitude. "It's just that this medication makes me feel like I'm outside of my body. Besides, I know that I am alright. I don't have mental illness like the doctors say." They all settle on the couch as Uncle Benjamin speaks. He says, "David. Son, we all agree with you and we are happy about that."

Finally, David has a calm moment with his family; that is, with most of his family. Bethany is missing in action, but this is nothing new. Since the other night, sightings of Bethany have been even more scarce. Nevertheless, David takes advantage of this uneventful moment with the family to express his gratitude. "Mama Netty, I really appreciated you coming out to see me almost every day. Even when they had me all spaced out. Don't get me wrong — I understand why I had to be on the medication. I was pretty messed up when I was admitted.

I couldn't always talk to you, but when you were there, I felt better. I felt safe. Did you know that the pastor came to see me a lot when I was in the treatment center?" Mama Netty puts on her 'matter- of- fact- voice' as she answers her grandson. "Yes, I made it my business to know everything pertaining to my favorite grandson while he was getting well." David laughs at his grandmother and says, "Grandma, I'm your only grandson." With that, Mama Netty adds, "And my favorite one."

Amber looks confused. "David. Why did you bring up the pastor? I'm just curious." David answers his sister with a bit of enthusiasm. "Oh, yeah, he helped me to get well. I mean, right now I can feel that weight is gone off my shoulders and chest. It was there for a long time and the longer it stayed, the heavier it got." He rolls his shoulders back and forth and takes a deep breath. "I feel free; that's the best way to describe it."

He returns to discussing the pastor and says, "He asked all the right questions. I could tell he was listening to me. He had me talking about things I

didn't even know I was thinking. I don't know —
the more I talked, the lighter I began to feel. It was
like I was emptying out. The doctors were calling it
bipolar, but I found that the more I talked it
through, the less angry I was. Then, I was able to
forgive Dad ..." He hangs his head down and shakes
it and then continues, "... and myself.

I realized that there was no need to be angry with
me because it wasn't my fault. It was after I realized
this that all the confusing thoughts began to
subside. The doctors were calling it schizophrenia,
but as I began to forgive Dad, Mama, myself... all
those voices went away. It got real quiet." He looks
at his family. "Actually, this was before they started
giving me all the medication. I just didn't know how
to express to the doctors that I was beginning to
feel better — that I was changing."

David gets quiet for a moment and then becomes
overwhelmed with an outpouring of emotional
gratitude. "Grandma, I'm okay...I'm really okay. I
thank God for what He's done. Uncle Benny, I'm
glad you're here. Amber, thanks for praying for me."
Then Mama Netty points out an important fact that

the rest of the family might not know. "Well, you know the doctors were very close to giving you medicine to treat schizophrenia-like symptoms, but since your mother allowed me to oversee your medical treatment with the doctors, I asked them to hold off on giving it to you. Instead we prayed."

And Amber, reflecting on her earlier conversation with Wendy, chimes in, "Yeah, our prayers gave the devil a black eye and hit him where it hurts!" David interjects, "Speaking of prayer. You know — this might sound weird, but the night I had my breakdown was the night the pastor prayed for me; right?" David Jr. takes a moment to see how the family is reacting to what he is saying and then he continues. "When he prayed for me, I felt like something changed. I don't know." He looks at his grandmother and asks, "Is it crazy if I say that the breakdown saved my life and the prayer had something to do with it?"

Amber doesn't give Mama Netty an opportunity to respond; instead, she cuts in and responds, "David, I don't think I have heard you talk this much since I've known you." He responds to his sister with a sentiment of freedom. "Well sis, you might as well get used to it because this is the real me. I mean, don't get me wrong, I still have some work to do emotionally, but I know I'm going to be alright."

And then with a sympathetic voice, he turns to Amber and speaks. "If you want to know anything about that day... if you have any questions sis, you can ask me. I don't mind talking about it now. I want you to be well too. If you need to know, just ask." Amber shrugs her shoulders and answers, "I really don't have any questions. I don't need to know. I know everything I need to know. I know my brother is going to be okay and that's enough for me."

"You know," Uncle Benjamin says to the three. "Thanksgiving is just a few days away and we have so much to be grateful for... so much." With this announcement, Mama Netty jumps to her feet, and in a frenzied state, begins to ready herself to leave. "Oh, that's right. Thanksgiving! So much had been going on around here that I forgot about Thanksgiving. We can't just let the holiday slip by without celebrating in a big way. We have to have a big dinner to thank God for His faithfulness. I'm going to have to get the Attaway sisters for help. Oh Lord, we got to get a turkey and a ham." She continues to build on the menu as she leaves out the front door.

The three just look at one another for a moment and then David speaks. "It's gone," he says. Curious, Uncle Benjamin inquires, "What's gone, David?" With a huge smile on his face, David responds, "The sadness, the grief. You know, I never looked forward to the holidays. Just the thought of holidays or if anyone mentioned a holiday, I always had this sad feeling come over me that I could never shake. I just noticed that it's gone." Uncle Benjamin comments, "That's great. All the more reason to celebrate big this Thanksgiving."

He begins to rise to his feet, but David stops him. "There is just one thing." Both Uncle Benjamin and Amber wait to hear what he has to say and he continues after a brief dramatic moment. "I wish Mamma could find the peace that I have found and that she could see just how much she has to be grateful for. Pastor Wynn says it like this ..." He attempts to impersonate his pastor as he says, "Taking on an attitude of gratitude adds latitude."

"Adds Latitude?" Amber asks. David proceeds to explain as he rises to his feet. "Yeah. Feet together," he says as he puts his feet together. "Stomach in," he says as he slightly tucks his tummy in. "Chest out," he says as he slightly sticks his chest out. "Smile." He holds his chin up and smiles. "Latitude! And Latitude is leeway for freedom from bondage of depression or anything that the devil tries to throw my way!" They both realize that he is standing straight up and down in a healthy, proud, confident manner and they both shout at the same time, "Latitude!" As Uncle Benjamin and Amber rise to their feet, Bethany enters through the front door. Immediately, the mood changes and so does the look on their faces.

Chapter Twelve

An Attitude of Gratitude adds Latitude

It's a few days later in the middle of a Tuesday afternoon. The door swings open and in comes Mama Netty and the Attaway sisters. Their arms are full of grocery bags and their voices are filled with holiday cheer as they begin to put the groceries away. Berlene goes through the bags she's just placed on the counter as she speaks.

"Well, I'm sure we have everything we need. A ham, turkey with all the trimmings, the ingredients for my green bean casserole, and my famous whipped potatoes, encrusted with bacon and cheese." Cherlene answers her sister with a strong objection. "Ah, you mean my famous recipe; don't you? Now, I will admit, Berlene, that you came up with the idea of putting hazelnuts and cranberries in the green bean casserole, but every

Thanksgiving, you wanna try and take credit for my whipped potato casserole..."

Berlene snaps back at her sister and says, "I take credit, because the Bible says to give credit where credit is due."

"Yes," Cherlene continues. "That's right, Berlene. The Bible does say to 'give' credit where credit is due. I don't see where it says to 'take' credit if credit is not due. You don't take credit if nobody gives you credit. It says to give, not take. That's just stealing and the Bible says, "Thou salt not steal... thy sister's recipe... or else... thou art damned to hell..."

Berlene is searching through the bags as she answers her sister, "Now, you know the Bible don't say all that Cherlene. You can have the recipe though because I have a new one anyway."

Meanwhile, Mama Netty has come across some mysterious items in a grocery bag that she is unpacking. As she reads the labels, she inquires, "What is ... preserved duck eggs?" She picks up another package, "...Cactus flower buds..." And another, "Shad roe sacks...who?" She looks at the sisters with a look of confusion. Berlene begins to move towards Mama Netty to rescue her items. "Oh, I'll take those. Did you come across the cow tongue yet?"

Cherlene looks at her sister with disbelief, "Berlene, this is not the time for a food network mystery basket contest... this is Thanksgiving with the Clearwaters. You know Mama Netty is very particular about her Thanksgiving menu. All the food has to be just right." She looks to Mama Netty for approval and agreement. "A festive menu for a festive holiday."

Mama Netty breaks in with a whimsical attitude. "And a Thanksgiving this is going to be. Yes, we are going to have the ham, the turkey and stuffing with all the trimmings ... but this year, the food is not what's going to make our Thanksgiving so special. This year, we're taking on an attitude of gratitude, and we're going to really celebrate our blessings in God."

Cherlene gives a quick side-eye to her sister as she answers Mama Netty. "Oh, I see Mama Netty, but we can still make the food really good; right? You know, because having dinner with your family is always entertaining..." Catching on to her sister's inference, Berlene adds her sentiments, "And good food is always better served with good entertainment."

The sisters share a laugh as Bethany walks through the door. Mama Netty continues with their conversation. "I know you are going to put a whole lot of love in this Thanksgiving and I appreciate you for that. But this year, let's just say we are going to do Thanksgiving right!"

Bethany overhears the end of this conversation and lets out a loud sigh. With a bit of anxiousness, she interrupts, "Oh, Netty. You're not planning a big dinner for Thanksgiving; are you? I wish you had consulted with me first. I've made reservations at the Crystal Dining Room for you all this year; my treat. I'm not feeling up to celebrating this year." She then extends an invitation to the sisters. "Oh, and I can add Berlene and Cherlene to your party if you like."

She turns to the sisters, eager to hear their confirmations to the invite. "Would you both like to join the family?" Mama Netty clears her throat in an authoritative way. While keeping her eyes on Bethany, she begins to instruct the Attaway twins. "Ah, Berlene and Cherlene. Gather all the groceries you need and take them with you to your house for Thursday morning. Oh, and we'll go tomorrow for all the desserts."

Cherlene answers, "Well, matter of fact, Mama Netty, we left most of the bags that we need out in the car." She gathers a few items from off the counter and tucks them into one of the bags that she is about to pick up. Berlene is busy searching through one of the bags. "Here, Cherlene; here's my cow tongue." She slips the package into one of the bags and begins to help her sister carry the bags out. "Good to see you, Bethany. You're looking good these days. I noticed you're plumping up a little; it looks good on you though." Berlene speaks to Mama Netty before leaving and says, "Netty, just give us a call later this evening. Meanwhile, should I go ahead and brine the turkey?" With her eyes still watching Bethany, she sternly nods her head in affirmation and they leave.

Without saying a word, Mama Netty gestures Bethany to join her at the sofa.

She speaks, "Now, Bethany, I've kept quiet long enough. I won't keep quiet any longer because it's time. It's time for change. I won't continue to stand by in silence, watching you destroy this family."

"Mama Netty, I..."

Mama Netty impatiently cuts her off. "Hush! I'm going to say what needs to be said and you're going to hear me and hear me well. You cannot keep walking around with this anger. It's the poison seeping out of your heart that's slowly killing you and the rest of us."

Bethany interjects, "Ma Netty, I'm not..."

Mama Netty continues to speak. "You're resentful that your life, thus far, hasn't turned out the way you planned for it to."

Bethany is not willing to have this conversation, so she objects. "Ma, will you stop?! I'm not angry... and I'm not feeling like having this conversation."

She hops to her feet in an attempt to leave, but Mama Netty grabs her by the hand and pulls her back.

"Bethany, the truth is, you are angry. You're angry that your husband died. You're angry your husband killed himself. You're angry you didn't know your mother or your father. You're angry that every time you look at your son, he reminds you of your dead husband ... who killed himself! You're angry that your sister is an alcoholic and that every time she comes around, she embarrasses you, plus, her mere presence invokes the pain you felt when you were handed over to foster care. You're angry that you had to work hard because life didn't deal you a good hand."

Bethany loses her patience with her mother-in-law and explodes with bitter anger. "And don't I have a right to be angry?! Don't I have a right?!" She stares at Mama Netty and waits for an answer. When she doesn't get one, she speaks again. "If I was angry, these would be good reasons; don't you think?" She tries to rise from the sofa again, but Mama

Netty puts a stern hand on Bethany's lap, preventing her from moving.

"There is a such thing as righteous anger and unrighteous anger. In these past eight years, your righteous anger has become something cruel and evil, punishing yourself and those who love you."

At this, Bethany becomes enraged.
"What!? Y'all got it good. Haven't I taken good care of you all?"

Mama Netty refuses to fall into the trap of offense and calmly answers Bethany.
"Bethany! You know what I'm saying. You need to face the truth so you can finally grieve."

With the same rage, she defends herself as she says, "I grieved... I wore black for a whole month."

Unmoved by Bethany's strong emotional anger, Mama Netty continues, "After David Sr. died, I watched you. I should have said something then. Almost immediately, you were busy making plans to start your business. You fully submerged yourself into those plans. At first, I thought that it was good for you, but then, I noticed how hard you were fighting."

Bethany snaps back at her, "Because that's what I do, I fight and I do not give up."
She seems to calm down a little. She takes a breath and then continues.
"How could I fight with so much pain? I needed to fight for me and for my children. Grief is pain; you can't fight and grieve at the same time."

Mama Netty continues as if she didn't hear Bethany.
"It was as if you were feeding off your own bitterness, resentment and anger to get the fuel you needed to succeed. But, Bethany, vengeance should never be a motive for success."
"Vengeance... who am I taking vengeance against?"
But Mama Netty continues to talk as if Bethany has not said a word.
"...in the process, it drove you to abandon your children and their emotional needs and even your own. Anger keeps you in denial, and in the end, the anger that you had every right to feel when your

world fell apart will become the very thing that will torment your soul."

Bethany begins to adjust herself on the couch. She folds her hands in her lap as a final sign to Mama Netty that she has conceded to this conversation. She begins to speak slowly and calculated.
"After David Sr. died, I wanted to die! I felt like my heart had been ripped out of me and I couldn't breathe. Every time I took a breath, I felt like I was dying again and again. I got to the point where I wanted to stop fighting. I didn't know what to do with the pain!"
She stops for a moment, then looks at Mama Netty, and speaks to her.
"I don't expect you to understand this."
She drops her head, struggles for a moment and then proceeds to let her thoughts out.
"... I drowned myself ... until I died in my pain..."
She glances up for a moment.
"It wasn't something that I had planned." She begins to explain. "One day, I got into my car and just started driving. I found myself in the middle of nowhere... at the Atlantic Ocean. I stood alone on the beachfront just before dusk."

Bethany thinks back to that night and continues to tell her story in a monotone voice.

"It was as if some force had summoned me there. Perhaps, it was God — perhaps, the devil; I don't know who. But I knew why I was there. I needed to be free from the pain, so that I could fight again!"

Again, she looks up at her mother-in-law.

"Truth makes you free; right? I needed to be free So, I pulled myself together and confronted truth. The truth was..."

She continues to stare at Mama Netty with sincerity in her eyes...

"David Sr., the love of my life, was dead; he wasn't coming back. He was gone. He chose to leave me and the children. Yes, I accepted that he had committed suicide. Everything in me knew that that was the truth. I had to accept that there wasn't enough fight in him to overcome. I accepted the truth that I knew something was wrong, but I didn't know what. I accepted the truth that even if I did know 'what', there was a good chance that things would have turned out the same. I accepted that I was not in control. I faced the truth that my dreams were shattered — my life altered forever. And what was the point in living this life as I knew it?"

"Bethany, you deferred your dreams," Mama Netty says in amazement.

Bethany responds without missing a beat and says, "David Sr. deferred my dreams…"

There is a long period of silence between the women; up until this point, Bethany has not shed a tear. But, now her eyes fill with water until the tears begin to roll down her face.

"And It was a painful death. With every truth that I had to accept, a part of me died. And I accepted my anger, my fears. I cried, I screamed, I cursed God, I cursed the devil and I cursed David's soul."

At this, Mama Netty lets out a gasp as she takes Bethany's hands up in her hands to plead with her daughter-in-law.

"What have you done? I get what you are telling me, but Bethany, you symbolically … or … in essence, died in your anger. You so called, died cursing God and playing with the devil." Mama Netty thinks to herself. "It makes sense now — the anger. Don't you know that the condition in which you end is the same condition in which you begin?

Bethany continues, "I didn't know what to do with the pain. I'm a fighter, and I didn't know how to fight the pain so I faced the truth and I died."
She looks at Mama Netty and pleads for her to agree with her.

"The truth made me free, Mama! I went to the edge of the water and I kept walking into deeper and deeper waters until I felt free of the pain. That night, in the ocean, I submerged myself in the darkness. I held my breath for as long as it took – because I knew that the very next breath I would take would be the breath of freedom. And when I came out of my oceanic grave, I had a new reality. A new life to make for myself. I died, David Senior's wife was dead and buried in her oceanic grave. My life as I knew it to be was gone."
She adjusts herself, squaring off her shoulders as she continues.
"So, I wiped my tears; I blew my nose ... and you're right. I began to reinvent my life on that very evening during the drive home. I would say that it is a mighty fine life I invented... wouldn't you?!"

Mama Netty shakes her head as she answers her.

"You made it... you did it. You've conquered the world. Ask yourself then: why am I not happy? You have a beautiful home and beautiful things — lovely children and a thriving business — money in the bank, and to hear you tell it, not a need in the world. You don't even need God, according to you." She looks her daughter-in-law directly in the eyes and asks once again, "Why aren't you happy?" She waits for a response and there is none and so she continues.

"What good is it for a man to gain the whole world but lose his own soul? You have to forgive... God, David Sr., your mother, father, your sister... and me."

"You? I don't have a reason to be mad at you." Mama Netty gives her daughter-in-law a look of resign.

"Maybe for what I'm getting ready to say. Bethany, you're selfish; you have become callous and indifferent. When are you going to get it that it's not all about you? It's not just about you and your comfort zone. You've turned into something I don't even recognize, and frankly, someone I don't like."

At these words, Bethany wants to remove herself from this discussion, so she begins to rise to her feet, but Mama Netty holds her down with a firm hand again. They sit in silence with Mama Netty waiting patiently for Bethany to speak. Finally, she does.

"I'm tired Mama Netty — really tired and I know I have to do things differently... for ..."
She stops abruptly, subconsciously holds her stomach and then she continues.
"I just don't know."

Mama Netty changes the mood.
"Nonsense; that's bologna... I've watched you fight and overcome against the odds. There's nothing Bethany Clearwater cannot achieve when she commits her heart and soul. I love that about you... I wish David Sr. was here to witness it; he would be proud."

At the mention of his name, Bethany throws her head back and closes her eyes in frustration.
"Oh, Mama; what have I done? What am I doing?"

Mama Netty once again takes her daughter-in-law's hands in her hands and begins to encourage her. "Bethany, there is always a chance for a new beginning. Only this time, you have to begin with your help."

She points to the sky and then gives Bethany an earnest look.

"Put down the boxing gloves and start trusting God again. You are a fighter, but you have lost your way."

She chuckles at her next thought before she can even get it out.

"You've got to take on an attitude of gratitude because, as David Jr. says, it adds latitude."

Bethany gives Mama Netty a seriously dumbfounded look and Mama Netty proceeds to explain the phrase, but Bethany cuts her off with her own thought.

"Mama Netty, I don't think I ..."

She cannot bring herself to say what she knows she needs to say, so she just gives up. "I'm just not feeling well."

"Here's the thing, Bethany." Mama Netty begins to close the conversation by getting to the point. "We are going to start living again. In a few days, we are going to gather together as a family — right here. We are going to feast on our Thanksgiving meal, but beforehand, we are going to count our blessings and renew our commitment of working together and loving one another as a family. We're going to give ourselves permission to make mistakes and to forgive one another when we do so. We are going to get through a family gathering without fighting and cussing one another out or reminding each other of our failures. If you don't feel that you're up to the challenge, then it's simple — just stay in your room. Either way, we will spend Thanksgiving reminding one another of just what we have to be grateful for."

Just then, the doorbell chimes ring out and Mama Netty gets up to answer the door. As she moves towards the door, Bethany blurts out what she's been trying to tell Mama Netty. "I'm pregnant. I've been trying to tell you that I'm pregnant." Mama Netty stops in the middle of her stride, turns to face Bethany and very calmly responds, "I know, Bethany; I know. It's a really good reason to start

over; don't you think?!" They stare at one another
with mutual affection and then Bethany motions to
Mama Netty, letting her know it's okay to answer
the door.

When she opens the door, a lively Mr. Thompson
comes striding in with a bright colored
bouquet of flowers in his hand. "Well hello, hello,
hello there. Netty, you ready to live a little tonight
on the town? A movie, dinner and a little dancing."
He dances hilariously for a few seconds, and in the
same motion, presents the bouquet of flowers to
Mama Netty. She gathers her handbag and gives
Bethany a comforting glance. She then joins Mr.
Thompson where he's stands waiting for her.

She takes the flowers out of his hand and tosses
them on the kitchen counter before they leave,
laughing and talking among themselves. After they
leave, Bethany reaches inside her handbag and
pulls out a business card. She reaches over to the
coffee table, picks up her cell phone and begins to
dial. "Hello, Pastor Mary? This is Bethany
Clearwater ... yes, I'm well; thank you. I'm
wondering if that offer for those counseling

sessions is still an option? Great, when can we get started?"

Chapter Thirteen

REPENTANCE BRINGS DELIVERANCE

Bethany and Pastor Mary Charleston are sitting on
the sofa talking. Bethany reaches over to the table
next to her and grabs the coffee kettle. She begins
to pour herself more coffee and then, she offers the
same to her guest. "Would you like a little more
coffee, Pastor?" Pastor Mary graciously responds as
she glances at her watch. "Oh, no thank you,
Bethany. As a matter of fact, we should probably be
wrapping this up in a little bit. I hope you see the
importance of meeting again and on a regular basis
for a while."

Bethany responds by bringing up an unanswered
question she'd asked earlier.
"Earlier, you asked if I felt like I've accepted that I'm
a widow. I would say yes. I accepted that on the day
they took my husband's lifeless body out of our
garage on a stretcher... in a body bag. It was black

— the color of death...the body bag was. You see? I'm not in denial."

Unmoved, Pastor Mary points out another potential issue.

"What about anger?"

They share a moment of silence and then Bethany responds with a smirk on her face. "I'm angry at the world and everything in it, to hear my mother-in-law tell it."

In the same calm manner, Pastor Mary begins to explain to Bethany.

"Anger is a human emotion and it's a necessary stage of the healing process. The Bible instructs us to be angry but to sin not. In other words, we will experience anger, but we should not let it rule over us. In times of great loss, to those who are grieving, anger can be used as a source of structure, helping us to remain functional. It can be used as an object of strength, helping us to maintain control over our lives. This is useful as long as your anger begins to dissipate within a reasonable period. However, repressed anger can..."

Bethany cuts Pastor Mary off with a blank stare on her face.

"I don't think I ever came up out of the ocean on that night. I think I stayed in that ocean, drowned myself in Thursday nights, Saturday mornings... my work, money... it was like I had been living in an underwater world..."

Bethany stops talking to look to Mary for an answer to what she just shared. But Pastor Mary has just two words for Bethany.

"And now?"

Bethany resumes sharing.

"And now? Now?"

She thinks for a long moment, and then she finds the words she was searching for.

"You know how you can jump in a swimming pool and swim underwater for as long as you can hold your breath? And when you come up and open your eyes, it takes a minute for you to get your bearings because you come up out of the water in a different place than you first entered. So, everything looks different. I've been living in an underwater world for so long, and now that I've come up for air... the whole scenery is different. I don't recognize anything... myself... my old life..."

Pastor Mary responds, "Sounds like you could have repressed anger."

Bethany thinks for a long moment, then she shares, "When we got married ... What we had most in common was love for one another. Our love language interpreted was, 'I got your back.' I live for you and you for me.' We wanted to conquer the world with our love. Our goal was to grow old together in love with the idea of loving others... family, community, friends. We loved life — both of us! Then, he chose to die."

"How does that make you feel?" Pastor Mary calmly asks.

"Betrayed! He lied; he had me fooled... he had me believing in love again?"

"Again?" Pastor Mary asks.

Bethany is enjoying this freedom to express herself and her answers are beginning to flow more freely.

"He took his life; he chose to abandon us, and I loved him so much. He didn't give me a chance to change my mind. I never fell out of love with him." Bethany begins to cry and this surprises her, but she continues to express herself.

"When you love someone, you love someone. You can't just change your mind. He changed his mind, or maybe, he never really loved me the way I needed him to. We didn't have the same definition for love. He was my hero."
She looks at Pastor Mary as she attempts to explain to her what she means.
"My sister handed me over to the state and then, I was alone. I loved her; she abandoned me, but she was my hero. Life lesson... Heroes let you down... so..."

There is a long silence and then Pastor Mary speaks.
"So?"
Bethany continues, "So, I became my own hero..."
"How's that working out for you?" Pastor Mary quickly asks.

After yet another long pause, Bethany responds.
"It was working just fine until..."
And again, Pastor Mary holds Bethany accountable
to her thoughts.
"Until?"

Pastor Mary has finally gotten Bethany to a mindset
of repentance, so Bethany resolves to come clean
with how she really feels.
"Let's just say that I know it's time for me to
denounce the deal I made with the devil. I want
myself back. I want to love again. I want to be free. I
want my children back. I want to look around and
for once see past this sea of abyss and truly
appreciate what I have. My son could be dead right
now, but he's not; he's doing well. I've been
pretending I don't care because I just don't know
how to feel anymore. I have a beautiful daughter
who has inherited all my strengths and ... she
doesn't even know how proud I am of her and she
wouldn't believe me if I told her. I want to become
their hero..."
She thinks to herself for a moment.
"It's ironic that the very ones I thought I was
fighting for are the very ones I've abandoned."

Neither of the women speak and then Pastor Mary's calm voice breaks the silence.

"Bethany, let me pray for you right now."
Pastor Mary moves toward Bethany to take her hands in her own and beckons her to stand up facing her.
"Dear heavenly Father, I bring this daughter before you. I ask you to look from heaven on her behalf and give her what she needs to walk through this next chapter of her life."
Pastor Mary stops abruptly and looks at Bethany with startled eyes.
Then continues, "Bethany, God just showed me you have been mad at Him. You turned your back on Him and cursed him... and that you have been wanting to come to Him again, but..."
And Bethany finishes the statement herself and says, "I just don't know how to."
Pastor Mary offers the solution, "Yes, He said that you must forgive. You have to forgive before you can get back to Him and when you do, He will reconcile and heal you and heal all your relationships. You must forgive... so say this prayer after me Bethany, and I need you to do so with a

sincere heart. God is here and He's listening." Tears begin to stream down Bethany's face as she begins to experience the presence of God. She takes over the prayer, smiling at Pastor Mary.

"I know He's here; I can feel Him again. Dear Lord, forgive me for turning my back on you; I do forgive you. I forgive David Sr., Savannah and anyone else that I need to forgive… even myself for abandoning my children."

Pastor Mary breaks in the prayer to coach Bethany on what to do next.

"That's good, Bethany. Now, denounce the evil you have been living."

Bethany agrees and begins to do so.

"It's true! I made a pact with the devil. Please forgive me for the life I have been living. I denounce this evil!"

Bethany begins to shake as a guttural scream comes out of her. She drops to her knees as she continues to scream as if a force from within her is escaping through her mouth. Pastor Mary continues to hold Bethany's hands tightly as Bethany shakes, jerks and continues to scream. It all happens pretty quickly. Suddenly, the screaming and jerking stops just as abruptly as they began. Pastor Mary helps Bethany up off the floor and leads her to the couch, and they sit as she begins to comfort Bethany.

"What just happened?!" Bethany asks. Pastor Mary proceeds to explain with the same calm voice, "Deliverance. Deliverance just happened. Bitterness, anger and rejection just left you. God heard your prayer and released you from the power of darkness. Now Bethany, anger and rejection will try to come back to you, but you must reject them. They can only stay if you give them permission to."

Bethany responds with an uneasiness. "I don't know if I'm strong enough to do that yet. So, I can honestly say that I do recognize that there is a need for me to continue to meet with you and I am ready to make the commitment." Pastor Mary responds with what just may be her first smile since they began.

"Wonderful!" she shouts. "Now, what I need you to do is one day next week, call my office and my assistant will put you on the calendar for a series of sessions. You will need to come to my office for these counseling sessions. I urge you, Bethany, to keep these appointments at all costs and in turn, you will find good progress."

Bethany finds peace and is a little more at ease upon hearing these instructions and confirms to Pastor Mary that she intends to follow her instructions. "Okay, great. I can do that." Pastor Mary continues to encourage Bethany. "Bethany just remember this: Rome wasn't built in a day. Please know that it's going to take some time. What's important for you is that you have a safe place to talk. I encourage you to begin to attend church on a regular basis... and just give it some time..."

Bethany becomes consciously aware of her pregnancy as she holds her belly. "I don't have too much time," she says. "This little one will be here and when she or he gets here, I want a happy home." "Well, congratulations." Mary gives her a reassuring smile. "You've taken the necessary steps. You are now on the road to happiness." She smiles back at Pastor Mary, taking notice that she's beginning to feel better already.

"You know; I feel that way. To be honest with you, just meeting with you for these few hours has been comforting. The one thing I can bring myself to admit is that I haven't been happy for quite some time." Pastor Mary takes her by the hands, looks at her in the face and says, "Happiness is a state of mind... Paul, the Apostle said, 'I have learned, in whatsoever state I am, therewith to be content.' I don't' want to come off religious because it's not about religion; it's about relationship.

Paul had grown into such a knowing and trusting relationship with Jesus that he could say, 'I can do all things through Christ which strengthens me.' He found contentment and happiness no matter what his lot in life served him... when he was full — whether he was empty or hungry — when he was lonely or had a good reason to be disappointed — when those close to him abandoned him, he found that the secret of living in every situation was his unshakable faith in the one who loved him the most.

Bethany, you are going to be okay; I promise. You just have to find your personal relationship with Christ, commit your life and family to Him and then begin to grow in your faith in Him. This is why I say, give it some time. Oh, yes, and try to attend church on a regular basis so that God can water the seeds He is planting in you." After she finishes, Pastor Mary begins to gather her things as Bethany talks to her. "I have to tell you, Pastor Mary, I certainly appreciate you coming out for a home visit. Quite frankly, if you hadn't agreed to come to me, I don't know if I would have had the courage to come to your office. And, thanks for listening on today without judging."

Pastor Mary proceeds to the door with Bethany following close behind her. "You are quite welcome," she responds. "And it was my pleasure to come over today. Bethany, I look forward to taking this journey with you. So, I will see you soon? Remember... give it..." And Bethany finishes Pastor Mary's statement with, "Some time; I know. Thanks again, Pastor Mary." They shake hands and afterwards, Pastor Mary embraces Bethany briefly before leaving out of the door. Bethany closes the door, walks back over to the couch, takes a seat and begins to weep.

Chapter Fourteen

IT'S A NEW DAY

It's Thanksgiving Day at the Clearwater household and the Attaway sisters are busy setting up for the day's festivities. Berlene is checking the pots on the stove and comes across her sister's 'misfit' dish. She takes the lid off and has an unfavorable reaction to the unpleasant aroma. "Cherlene, I don't know why you had to make this cow tongue concoction! Tell me again what cactus flower buds and fish sacks have to do with Thanksgiving? Besides, it smells a little off."

Her sister is busy at the dining room table making final adjustments on the table settings. She remains focused on the details as she responds to her twin. "Berlene, I've told you... they have nothing to do with Thanksgiving. I just wanted to step outside of the box... you know — live a little — as Netty has been saying lately. Something to change things up.

Besides, if you give it a try, you might find that you like my little side dish concoction."

Berlene snaps back obviously annoyed at her sister. "Anyway, will you set this centerpiece on the table and then I think we are ready to serve Thanksgiving dinner?" She glances at her watch, and says, "And just in time; they should be home in just a few minutes." Cherlene takes up the centerpiece and goes to place it in the middle of the table. She stands back to get a full view of their work.

"Berlene, all the food is delicious and the table looks good too. We outdid ourselves again. You think we'll have some good entertainment to go along with our efforts?" Berlene stops what she's doing and compassion fills her heart as she thinks about the Clearwaters. She responds, "Cherlene, to be honest with you, I'm hoping the entertainment will be a little different this time. It's about time for this family to experience some joy…. don't you think?"

Her sister quickly agrees with her. "Yes, I think so too… after what they went through that last time." She stops where she is standing, puts her hands on her hips and shakes her head. "That had to be the worst time ever." Then, she chuckles a little and jokes, "But it was good though. I think I ate a whole cake spectatoring that event. The gun show was colorful..."

Berlene cuts her sister off to correct her. "First, Cherlene, a teenager wielding a gun in the middle of his family gathering is nothing to laugh about. You could have been a victim of that gun show. You know that was a real bullet; don't you?" She half waits for her sister's response before moving on to her next point. "Secondly, Spectatoring?! Cherlene, is that even a word? That's not a word; you always trying to invent something. First you come up with this cow tongue, flower-fish egg nonsense that does not even resemble any traditional holiday dish, and now you want to change the English language..."

Berlene remains unmoved by her sister's rant. "You know it's not that serious, Cherlene." Then, she defends her choice of words, "The word is a word because..." She searches for a witty answer to give to her sister, but doesn't find one. "Well, because I just used it as a word! Furthermore, my dish has a name; it is a casserole! Casseroles are traditional dishes for any occasion." She changes her tone just a little and says, "But now Berlene, you do have a point. I hope the Clearwaters can get through the evening without a brawl... but just in case."

With that, she pulls out a huge bag of popcorn from under the kitchen counter and puts it on display for her sister to see. "I brought a little something extra for the show." They both begin to laugh until they see Mama Netty, Mr. Thompson, Uncle Benjamin, Savannah, Amber, and David Jr. arriving home from morning service.

The family goes into the living room to lounge before dinner. Mama Netty heads right to the kitchen and begins to lift the lids to take a peek at the good-looking food. "What's that smell in here?" Her hand lands on the cow tongue casserole; she lifts the lid and puts her nose close to the pot. Berlene and Cherlene have been beaming with pride up until this moment. They share a panicked glance at one another until the moment after Mama Netty renders her decision about the dish.

"Smells good... just like Thanksgiving is supposed to smell." Amber chimes in as she takes a walk through the dining area. "It looks pretty too." Mama Netty congratulates the sisters with an energetic smile. "Berlene and Cherlene you outdid yourselves this time." "Well when can we eat?" Mr. Thompson complains, "I'm starving. Listening to that Thanksgiving message worked up an appetite in me something awful."

Mama Netty responds to Mr. Thompson as she makes her way to the family room where everyone is lounging. "Well, I don't know how, after all, the pastor didn't mention food in his message this morning." Uncle Benjamin is quick to explain this dilemma. "But he sure had us standing and sitting — and sitting and standing — and lifting up our hands. It was like Jesus aerobics up in there..."

Mr. Thompson bursts into laughter as he agrees. "Thank you! I'm glad I'm not the only one who thinks so. But you know I really did enjoy the message... 'Putting on an Attitude of Gratitude'... and that latitude explanation..." David Jr. points out a rare occasion that took place in the morning service. "And Mr. Thompson, you didn't even fall asleep."

"Son, the message was good in all..." Mr. Thompson puts a little humor in his voice as he finishes his statement, "... but I really do think the credit goes to the Jesus aerobics." "Well," Mama Netty warns, "Your stomach is just going to have to hold its peace. We have just a few more people joining us for dinner today. We have the pastors, Mr. Winston and ..." She looks toward Bethany's bedroom, "... possibly..."

Savannah catches on to the possibility that Bethany will not be joining the family and gets excited. "What?! She-wolf is not going to be joining us for dinner?" But she is a little too happy about that for Mama Netty, so she gets corrected. "Now, Savannah, we will have none of that today. You have to be nice and mind your manners. If Bethany should choose to join us today, I'm counting on you to not provoke her."

Amber jumps to her feet and playfully adds a reminder to Mama Netty's correction as well. "Yeah

Auntie. You heard the pastor talking about practicing the fruit of the Spirit. Love, joy, peace, patience, kindness, goodness, faithfulness, gentleness and... self-control. So, no strong drink today either..." In the same playful tone, Savannah answers her niece. "Little missy, mind your own business. You just need to be grateful that I made it to church this morning. I can't promise what will happen after church hours." Amber gives her aunt a look of warning and then the two share a laugh.

The doorbell chimes ring out and gets the attention of every family member present, mainly because most are hungry and they are hoping that everyone that they are waiting on is behind the door. The Attaway twins respond first. At the same time, they say, "It's open!" Of, course, as always, they point to one another and each shout, "Jinx!"

In walks Winston with two bottles of Apple Cider Champagne. Mama Netty, who has one eye on Bethany's bedroom door, is the first to greet him. "Well, come on in and join in the fun. Glad you could make it, Mr. Winston." "I'm happy I could make it and thank you for having me, Mama Netty." He holds the bottles in each hand over his head and says, "I brought a few bottles of Champagne..." Savannah immediately begins to make her way towards the bottles, but Mr. Winston quickly explains, "... that's non-alcoholic Champagne." Amber giggles at her aunt as she embarrassingly returns to her seat. "What?! I knew that."

Winston makes his way to David Jr. and greets him with a manly handshake. "David, it's good to see you. How are you doing?" Before David can respond, he makes his way to Uncle Benjamin and greets him with the same handshake, and then on to Mr. Thompson. The entire family spontaneously begin to go around the room hugging and shaking hands and wishing one another a happy Thanksgiving.

Amid this show of benevolence for one another, the doorbell chimes again and the Attaway twins are the only ones who actually hear it. They fall into their habit of speaking at the same time and then shouting "jinx" at one another. In the next moment, Pastors Wynn and Mary Charleston walk in and begin to join in with the same greetings.

After a few moments, Mama Netty gets everyone's attention, as she
continues to glance at Bethany's bedroom door. "Okay, so we are just about ready to feast, but before we sit down to dinner this year, there is something we all must do. I want us to count our blessings this year. So, we are going to go around the room and each of us will express why we are grateful." She looks at Pastor Wynn with reverence and says, "Pastor, please give us the honor — be the first to indulge in our new family tradition."

He responds graciously, "It would be my pleasure." He takes his wife's hand. "First of all, I'm grateful to God for seeing fit to rescue me." He affectionately looks at his wife and says, "My lovely wife. I'm grateful for the gift that God gave me when He gave me you. You are my lover, my best friend, my help... it is an honor to do life and ministry with you."

Pastor Mary responds, "Well... of course I'm grateful for my husband who also just happens to be my pastor." She looks at him with the same affection that he displayed to her. "It's an honor to be your partner in life. You love so passionately and

selflessly, and for that, I am grateful to God."
Bethany appears out of her bedroom. She and
Pastor Mary lock eyes as she continues, "… and for
new beginnings, for the opportunity God gives us to
start fresh."

Mama Netty sees Bethany and motions her to come
near. Berlene goes next. "I'm thankful for my health
and my new hairstyle and for being here today. I'm
grateful for my sister, Cherlene, who has been with
me my entire life. Cherlene, I just want to say I
appreciate you." And next is Cherlene.

"This was a good idea, Mama Netty… I'm grateful
for the opportunity to tell others what I'm grateful
for. My sister and best friend: sometimes you get on
my nerves because you can be bossy and
aggravating… but I thank God for the sister bond
that we have. I can't imagine life without having
had a twin sister."

Mr. Thompson clears his throat and when he begins
to speak, it's clear that he's a little choked up and
dewy eyed. "I'm grateful for the Clearwater family,
who is really the only family I got." He turns to

Mama Netty and says, "Netty, I don't think I have ever said it, but thank you for adopting me as part of your family. If it weren't for y'all, I'd be one lonely man..." He takes a moment to change his mood and he looks more like a boy with his first crush. "I'm grateful for you going out on the town with me the other night." He quickly adds, "Uhhh — don't worry, Pastor; we kept it holy."

The family enjoys a comic relief moment and then, he continues. "Netty, I hope you had a good time because I sure would be forever gracious if you would agree to go out with me again..." Blushing, Mama Netty responds, "Why, I would be ever-so-gracious for the opportunity. I haven't felt that alive in years... and for that, I'm grateful to God and to Mr. Thompson...Thank you." She turns to the rest of the family and says, "I'm thankful to God for His faithfulness, for answering prayers and for these pastors who have prayed prayers for my family that have availed much. I'm grateful for health, healing and deliverance for my grandson, and I'm grateful for the beautiful and wise granddaughter that I have... I'm grateful for you, Bethany, and there is not a day that goes by that I do not give God thanks for keeping you when you became a widow..."

She takes a moment and looks at Bethany with an empathetic look and then turns her affection towards her son. "I'm grateful for my loving son who has been a source of strength and comfort in these hard times. Thank you, son." She takes a moment to catch her breath. "What I'm most thankful for this year is what God is going to do in this family in this next year." She takes Savannah's hand in hers. "I can see that He is setting the stage to mend relationships and restore the love that was lost."

It's Savannah's time to go next and her eyes have begun to water. "Don't get me to crying. I'm just thankful to the Lord for keeping me; it's been a hard road. I'm grateful for life." Uncle Benjamin speaks up next and says, "I'm grateful for my little brother's legacy living on through his children ... and for his wife who is a survivor." David Jr. speaks up with vigor and authority, which is quite impressive for a teenager. "I'm thankful for this Thanksgiving holiday. I'm glad to be alive and well... and I'm grateful for my mother, who has worked so hard to give us the best possible life, and for God helping her to do it."

Amber takes center stage to chime in next. She adds, "I'm thankful for my family, especially for Mama Netty, who has been a mother and grandmother and father and friend to me... Mama Netty... I love you. Thank you for your guidance and for making sure I met Jesus. I'm grateful that my brother is here today and in good spirits, and I'm grateful for my mother for all her sacrifices."

She looks at her mom and displays an affection she has not displayed toward her in quite some time. "Thanks Mom for not giving up." Bethany reluctantly clears her throat and begins to speak. "I guess it's my turn. Well, I'm grateful." She thinks, but can't find the words, so she begins again as the family looks on obviously cheering for her. "I'm grateful... for the hope that's in today. I'm thankful for truth... because truth makes you free... I'm grateful for love because it looks past faults... it forgives and disregards the offenses of others... I'm grateful to God for sticking with me, even when I turned my back on Him. I'm grateful ... just so grateful."

Mama Netty is getting ready to ask the pastor to bless the table, but realizes Winston hasn't gone. "Oh, there is one more... Mr. Winston, come on and don't be shy. Tell us what you are grateful for today." He begins, "In listening to you all, I guess I do take a lot for granted. I have a lucrative career, my health and good friends. Very seldom do I stop and thank God for the life that He has afforded me to live, but today, I want to thank Him."

He looks at Mama Netty and then towards Bethany. "I'm grateful for having been invited here today because I'm reminded of just how good I have it, but I just realized what is missing out of my life. He looks around the room and his eyes fall on Bethany. He continues to look at her as he continues, "What's missing is that relationship I once had with Him." He looks up toward Heaven and then at the pastor. "... and today, I'm making a commitment to come back to my first love. Pastor, you will see me at church on next Sunday."

Bethany gives him a faint smile of approval and someone begins to sing the song, "Give thanks with a Grateful Heart" and eventually, they all join in as they gather around the dining table. The Attaway Sisters begin to bring the food out and place it on the table. They continue to sing until the pastor's voice can be heard as he begins to bless the food. "Dear heavenly Father. We are gathered in your name today. We thank you for family and friends and healthy relationships. We thank you for the many blessings you have bestowed upon us... for every good and perfect gift is from above, coming down from the Father of the heavenly lights, who does not change like shifting shadows. We ask you to bless this food and the hands who have prepared it... and bless this time of fellowship just the same."

Chapter Fifteen

OH BABY, IT'S PROM

It's seven months later and it's Senior - Junior prom night for Amber and Wendy. Wendy is standing in the Clearwaters' living room. She's in front of a mirror taking selfies as she waits. She is dressed in a red formal gown, which could be a larger version of Bethany's gown from the Mayor's ball. It's been several minutes since her arrival, so she is getting a little impatient as she waits. "Now, they know they need to come on. We're going to be late getting to the prom." She catches a glimpse of herself in the mirror and freezes in that position. "Now, I know I look good. Did I get a picture of this side?"

She begins to snap another series of selfies. "Come on, y'all; we need to take pictures so that we can get on our way." She raises her voice to make sure she's heard. "I don't want to be late to our prom." A very handsome David Jr. appears dressed in a tux with his jacket in his arms. "Calm down, Wendy; you know the prom can't start without you." He steps back to look at his sister's best friend. "You look beautiful."

"Why thank you, David, for noticing. You clean up well yourself." Wendy prepares to take a selfie of the two of them and David poses with a smile before she snaps the picture. "You know, I wanna thank you for taking us to the prom." David objects. "How many times are you two going to thank me? It's my pleasure. Besides, there are no boys in school or in this entire district that are good enough to accompany my sisters to their prom." Wendy prepares for another selfie and they both smile and pose again.

Mama Netty and Uncle Benjamin enter the room at the same time. Mamma Netty, dressed in a bathrobe, emerges from down the hall and Uncle Benny from the front door. Uncle Benjamin has a bag with two arm corsages for the girls. Mama Netty doesn't waste any time doting over David Jr. "Oh, look at my favorite grandson... handsome... handsome indeed... I'm one proud grandmother...

uh where is your tie? Don't those suits come with ties?" David Jr. pulls an untied bow-tie out of his pocket and holds it up.

"No, but Mom bought me a bow-tie. Do I have to wear it though? I couldn't get it tied." Uncle Benjamin beams with pride as he comes to his nephew's rescue. "This is a job for your uncle, Benny. I'll have you know that back in the day, I was the bow-tie king. At my senior prom, I had the baddest bow-tie...to go along with my afro ... picked just right and my powder blue suit."

Mama Netty clears her throat, preparing to cut her son short of his bragging rights. "Uh, as I recall... you needed a little help with that first tie-it-yourself bow-tie since you had just graduated from the bow-tie clip-on club." Uncle Benjamin takes the 'call out' with stride as he continues to focus on tying his nephew's tie. "Uh, proving that everyone needs a little help every now and again." He finishes up tying the bow-tie and takes a proud look at his nephew. "Well, David Jr., God has certainly turned our grief into joy."

Mama Netty steps back for another proud look and then begins to fumble with her phone to take a picture. Meanwhile, Wendy has captured the entire intimate moment on her cell phone video. Winston comes through the front door with a small bag in hand and Mama Netty finally thinks she has her camera figured out. "Okay, let me see your pearly whites for the camera." She tries to snap the picture, but to no avail. "Benjamin, what's wrong with this thing?! See if you can work this camera. What button do I push again?"

Instead, Winston pulls out his camera. "I'll tell you what; how 'bout I take a group shot? Come on everyone, stop what you're doing and strike a pose for the camera for a second. We don't want to lose not one of these cherished moments... let's capture it on the count of three ... one... two..." Amber hurriedly comes into the living room shouting, "Photo bomb... strike a pose," and as she joins the group, Winston snaps the picture and then says, "... three." As they continue to pose for Winston's camera, a very pregnant Bethany steps into the living area.

"Okay, stay right there." Winston takes a few more shots and then turns his attention to Bethany. "Great. Now Bethany, come on and get in here. Stand in between the girls." "Is there room for this big belly? I really think I need to sit out on these series of pictures." She gives Winston a wink and a nod and says, "I'll just find a good seat over here on this here sofa. Don't mind me while I get comfortable right here." She gently backs to the edge of the sofa and slowly lowers herself down to take a seat.

"How you feeling, Mamma? You alright?" David asks as he moves to the couch where his mother is sitting. "I'm fine, David. You look so handsome. Can you sit here with me for a moment? I have something I want to show you." He takes a seat right next to her on the sofa. Bethany pulls a beautiful watch out of her pocket and puts it in her son's hand. The rest of the family gathers around.

"You have grown up to be such a jewel in this family. Matter of fact...." She glances up to find Amber with her eyes; she looks at her and then back at David. "You and your sister both have always been my jewels. I was in a dark place there for a while and I sort of forgot about what was always so important to me...my family." She tenderly caresses his hands. "Just a few short months ago, I almost lost you forever. I'm so grateful for the grace of God. I never would have been able to sit here and tell you how much I love you and your sister."

She focuses her eyes on Amber again to signify that she's talking to both children. "I know you have forgiven me, but I want to take this time out to acknowledge that you have forgiven your father too... well, that we have forgiven your father." She takes the watch out of his hands and holds it up to show it to the rest of the family as she continues making her presentation. "This watch was your father's, David Sr. — a good man who came across some tough times. We can never truly know why he chose to do what he did."

She glances down at the floor, but then looks up towards Heaven. "I have come to understand that sometimes in life, we don't have all the answers, but there are a few things I do know about David Sr."

She takes a moment to look at each of her family members before continuing. "One is that he was sure proud of his family... and this watch. It was presented to him out of appreciation from his colleagues at the bank when he made vice president." She looked at David Jr. with a warm smile and says, "I also know that if he were here today, he would've taken this day to express to you just how very proud he is of the young man you have become."

In her silence, she enjoys a good eye full of her handsome son. Her eyes fill up with tears of pride as she takes a moment to adjust his bow-tie, and then she continues. "Actually, there are several special items of your father's I have held onto for you both, which in time, you'll receive." She begins to slip the watch on his wrist. "This watch... it represented to him accomplishment. I've chosen today to present this to you because in these short few months, you have overcome so much. David Jr., don't stop. You have all of your father's strengths."

She leans over and pecks her son's cheek with a kiss. "And when you look at this watch, I want you

to remember that your father was a great man —
just like you are becoming. There is nothing you
can't achieve." Bethany gives her son a meaningful
hug as all the family tries to fight back tears. "Now, I
also know that he would have cherished the
opportunity to teach his son how to tie a bow-tie."
She quickly pulls the tie loose and begins to retie it.
Mama Netty and Uncle Benjamin share a laugh as
the rest of the family begin to celebrate the
moment.

Mr. Thompson enters through the front door,
announcing himself. He's overdressed, wearing a
tux with a tail and a chauffeur's hat on. "Mr.
Thompson at your service. Is everyone ready to go
to this prom?" He cuts his corny dance move while
Winston captures memories on video. Wendy, who
is busy touching up her makeup, has a strong
objection. "Wait a minute... he's going to our prom?!
I thought we hired a limo service."

Mr. Thompson takes offense to her objection and is
quick to tell her. "Now looky here, missy. I will have
you to know I have my CDL license. I can drive a
limo, a taxi, and even a bus." Just then, with a

complaining moan, Amber voices her objection as well. "Mom, is this your way of sneaking a chaperon with us?" Before Bethany can respond, Mama Netty speaks up. "Okay, calm down everyone... it's my fault... it was my idea... actually..."

Mama Netty takes off her bathrobe to reveal a beautiful blue formal dress." Amber objects again, "You too?! Mama Netty, we don't need chaperons." She looks to her Mom to plead her case. "Mom, I thought we settled this!" "Granddaughter," Mama Netty interjects in a calm, cool and collected tone. "I'm sorry, but me and Mr. Thompson have better places to go. No chaperons here; we are just dropping you off tonight and then, we will be on our way to... ah..." She quickly looks at Mr. Thompson. "Where are we headed to, Mr. Thompson? By the way, you sure look mighty dapper tonight."

Mr. Thompson looks at Mama Netty and begins to flirt as if they were the only two in the room. "Did I ever tell you that my favorite color is powder blue in formal wear? Netty, you got it going on tonight. We are headed to ... well, let's let it be a surprise...

but I will give you a hint... it's not the Junior/Senior prom." They both begin to laugh as he takes her by one hand and gives her a twirl so all can see his most beautiful girl in the world.

Meanwhile, Uncle Benjamin goes to the kitchen to pull the corsages out of the boxes. Winston has captured every cherished moment with his camera. "Well, you kids had better be getting on your way. We want you to enjoy every bit of your prom." As he approaches the girls with the flowers, he enlists his nephew's help for another special moment. "Now, little ladies, come on over here. David come help me with this." He gives one of the corsages to David and motions for him to pin it on Wendy, and he begins to present Amber with the other.

"Amber, you know your father would have loved this honor. He would've been proud of the fact that you were brave enough to invite your baby brother to the prom, rather than have a real date." David objects, "Heeey, I am a real date...Aren't I a real date, Wendy?" Wendy reassures him, "Sure, David. You sure are." Uncle Benjamin continues his intimate moment with his niece.

"Anyway... I am honored to have the honor to send you off to your first prom." He finishes his task and then stands back to get a good look. Soon after, he is overcome with emotion. "Have fun, baby girl. My baby niece all grown up and so lovely and pure. I'm proud... this is a proud moment." He embraces her.

"Thank you, Uncle Benny. I'm glad you are here too. I'm glad all my family is here."
Winston hands his video camera to Bethany and gives her brief operating instructions.
"Just one more thing — if you don't mind." He slips his hand into the bag he brought with him and carefully pulls out a boutonnière. "I took the liberty to pick this up for you, David. Do you mind?" He motions for permission to put it on David and David complies by coming to stand in front of him. He begins to pin the boutonnière on his lapel.

"Just be a man tonight young man. Watch out for your sisters... and have some fun... all of you." David looks at Mr. Winston square in his face and says, "Thank you Mr. Winston; it's pretty thoughtful of you." They exchange handshakes, but then, resolve to a hug. Bethany speaks with her face hidden behind the camera. "No kidding gang... you need to be on your way." Mr. Thompson takes this as his cue to show the teenagers and Mama Netty to the limo. "Well, you ready to get this party started...Mr. Thompson's Limo — at your service." He performs a perfect royal bow and motions his guests to the door.

Amber, Wendy and David pose for one last selfie with Wendy's phone camera. They then kiss and bid farewell to Uncle Benjamin, Bethany and Winston. They begin to laugh and celebrate as they make their way to the door and into the car, taking selfies along the way.

At their departure, the house becomes silent again. Uncle Benjamin promptly excuses himself. "Well, it's been a long day, and besides, I still have some packing to do. You know my flight leaves out tomorrow afternoon. Winston, you will be able to take me to the airport; won't you? Winston is delighted to set his mind at ease. "Absolutely. It's all taken care of, Uncle Benjamin. Don't you worry about a thing. I have your flight info so just be ready, and I will be here to get you there in plenty of time."

He starts on his way towards the guestroom. "Thanks a million, Winston. Bethany, I will see you in a little bit. You look a little flushed. You feeling okay? That little one is not on the way; right?!" He doesn't give much thought to his question and doesn't stay around for the answer; he simply continues down the hallway. "I'm going to finish packing and then, take a little nap."

Winston takes a seat next to Bethany where she has been sitting on the sofa. He looks at her and winks before speaking.

"Well, it's just you and me kid."

He settles all the way back into a lounging position on the sofa with his feet fully stretched out on the floor. There is silence as he crosses his ankles and begins to wiggle his feet from side to side. He breaks the silence without looking at Bethany. "Bethany, have you thought anymore about my marriage proposal?"

Bethany takes a deep breath and blows it out slowly before answering.

"Winston, as much as I would like to marry you, I just think that now is not the time. I kind of like where I am."

She takes another deep breath and blows it out slowly and continues.

"I'm enjoying this process."

Winston answers her with a tone of resolve in his voice.

"Well one thing I can say is that you certainly proved me wrong."

Bethany is a little confused.

"What do you mean? What are you talking about?"

He immediately responds, "Remember when I said, that I could help you to turn your house of misery into a house of joy again? Well, you proved that you didn't need my help for that." With a proud look on his face, he continues, "Bethany, you don't cease to amaze me. Nothing has given me more joy than to watch you gain your joy back."

Bethany rubs her very pregnant belly with both hands in a circular motion and takes another deep breath. She exhales slowly before speaking again.

"But Winston, you were right. You have helped me get my joy back. Your support and encouragement in these past months have been a tremendous comfort and help. I couldn't have..."

She glances at her belly, takes another deep breath then continues to talk while slowly exhaling.

"We couldn't have done it without you .... Besides, I think I'm truly blessed to have you in my life. You are truly a good man. You stuck around for me and my children. You didn't abandon us... for that, I'm forever grateful." She grits her teeth and distorts her face in pain, but she continues trying to keep her voice calm.

"One day, one day Winston Avalon... but today, I need you to do me a favor..."

Winston is still in his relaxed position on the sofa. By this time, he's sitting with his head laid back and his eyes closed as he is enjoying this quiet moment with Bethany.

"Your wish is my command. What is it my lovely lady? What can I help you with?"

Bethany lets out a bit of a yelp and begins to breathe a little deeper and faster.

"Winston... I need you to... get me to the hospital because I'm in labor... this little one is ready to come out..."

Upon hearing this, Winston springs to his feet and begins to stir around like a chicken with its head chopped off.
"Are you sure? How long have you been in labor?"
In between breaths, Bethany tries to get his attention. She responds as she reaches for him to help her up off the sofa.

"Pretty much the whole day... I just didn't want to say anything because I know the kids wanted to be there for the birth. I just couldn't take this day away from them... Did you see their faces? But right now ... I got to go..."
She lets out a yelp and follows it with a long moan.
"Well, alright."

Still in a frenzy, Winston begins to search for his keys. He looks in the direction of the kitchen, and then, where he was sitting on the sofa. He finally locates them in his front pocket.
"What are we waiting for?"

He gently helps Bethany to her feet as he continues to nervously ask her questions.

"We had better get going; where are we going? Did you call your doctor? Where is your bag? Are you ready to go?"

Bethany points to the corner at her bag as she picks up her cell phone from the coffee table.

"Okay, I'm calling my doctor now. I'm ready to go." They head for the door and Winston abruptly stops as if he's forgotten something.

"Should we tell Uncle Benjamin?"

Between shallow, panting breaths, Bethany shakes her head.

"No, let him nap... he's not going anywhere tomorrow... he will be here for a while... I told you he always wears out his welcome when he comes to visit."

Bethany lets out a few screams as they scurry out of the door.

Chapter Sixteen

JOY!

It's five months later and another Thanksgiving Day
at the Clearwater house. The Attaway sisters are in
the kitchen and dining room area busy preparing
for the festivities of the day. Savannah is sitting on
the sofa, drinking a soft drink and talking on her
cell phone. "Alright… yes, everything is ready." She
looks over her shoulder into the dining area, "I
believe we are just waiting on everyone to get here.
Okay. We'll see you then. Goodbye."

She ends the call and begins to talk with the sisters.
"That was Mama Netty. She said to get the food
ready for serving. They are just a few minutes
away." The sisters speak at the same time.
"Everything is ready." They stop, look and point at
one another. "Jinx. We are just waiting for
everyone." They point to one another again and

then say, "Jinx." Savannah looks over her shoulder to the sisters and shouts in frustration, "Will y'all stop with that jinx stuff already?! Goodness! You've been doing it all day! Is that a twin thing or what?! It's driving me up the wall. Besides, don't y'all know that's voodoo black magic stuff?! Jeez, you both been going back and forth putting curses on one another. I'm sorry I was late getting here and missed my ride to church. Y'all make me need the gospel!" After a moment, she looks over her shoulder at the twins again and gives them one last warning on the subject, "... and you both will need the gospel too if you don't stop with all that nonsense."

Bethany enters from her bedroom, talking on her cell phone and carrying a baby girl wrapped in a pretty pink blanket. She walks straight to Savannah and sets the baby in her lap. Bethany speaks to Savannah while still on the phone, "Here. Take your niece... please..." She goes back to her phone conversation. "Yes, Winston, we will wait for you, but just don't be too long getting here." She disappears back into her bedroom.

"Yes, I will hold my niece; won't I, Gracie-Joy?" Savannah immediately perks up and begins to have baby-talk with her niece. "My pretty little niece... hello you... Gracie-Joy... you see Auntie..." Berlene and Cherlene stop what they are doing and each have a confused look on their face. Berlene speaks up first. "Savannah, why you call that baby Gracie? Her name is Joy Elizabeth Clearwater..."

Cherlene, cuts her sister off and sympathetically scolds Savannah. "Yeah. Where you get Gracie from? You're going to have her confused when she gets older...she won't know her name." Savannah answers the sisters in the same baby-talk voice, "I have my reasons... besides, look at this beauty; doesn't she look like a Grace?" She holds the baby up so the sisters can get a good look at the smile forming on her face. They are melted by the smile. They race to where Savannah is sitting with the baby and join her in her baby-talk with Joy.

Several minutes have gone by and Mama Netty, Mr. Thompson, Uncle Benjamin, Amber, David and Wendy arrive home. Mama Netty greets the ladies and then Joy in the same baby-talk voice as the ladies. "Hello you all. Hello little Joy; you are so pretty in your pink — yes you are." Then, in her regular adult voice, barks orders at the family. "Everyone, don't go too far off now. Before we eat, we must gather for our Thanksgiving tradition as soon as the pastors arrive." She turns to Savannah and asks, "Is Bethany here?"

But Cherlene and Berlene answer at the same time. "She's in her room." They point to one another, but they both see the look on Savannah's face and decide to forego their ritualistic 'jinx.'" Satisfied with the answer, Mama turns her attention to Savannah. "You missed a wonderful service this morning. What happened to you?" Without taking her eyes off her niece, she answers the question with a tinge of disappointment in her voice. "I missed my bus. What was the message?"

Mama Netty becomes energized and animated as she begins to review the morning message. "The title of pastor's message was 'Be Grateful for God's Joy.' He used the scripture, 'Weeping may endure for a night, but joy cometh in the morning. Let me tell you something... he tore that church up; you hear me? Berlene — Cherlene — I'm going to get the CD for y'all… it was good." She turns to the rest of the family and asks, "Wasn't it, y'all?" Just then, the doorbell chimes ring out. Mama Netty starts for the door, but Bethany darts across the floor, headed to the door before she can take a step. She opens the door and tries to hide her disappointment. "Oh. Hello Pastors Wynn and Mary; come on in. I'm so sorry. I was expecting Winston. She motions with her hands and opens the door wider, giving them room to enter. "Please come on in." They enter and begin to greet everyone.

Before Bethany can shut the door, she spots Winston walking up the driveway. "What in the world?! Oh, my…"
Everyone stops what they are doing to look at Bethany. "What's wrong, Mom?" Amber asks as she looks up from smiling at her baby sister. Uncle Benjamin goes over to where Bethany is standing to see for himself what Bethany sees. He sees what she sees and immediately takes on the same flabbergasted facial expression as Bethany.

In a frustrated tone, Amber inquires of her mom again. "Mom, is everything okay? Mama Netty chimes in with a little impatience. "Well Bethany; tell us something. What is it? Benjamin?" Finally, while keeping her eyes fixed ahead, a big smile appears on her face. She answers, "Everything is okay... everything is fine... it's just Winston."

At that, Winston bursts through the door, pulling a bunch of gold balloons overhead and a beautiful bouquet of flowers tucked under one arm. In each of his hands, he holds a bottle of Apple Cider Champagne, and between his lips, a sign that reads in big bold letters, "She said yes." As he steps in, Uncle Benjamin begins to relieve him of some of the items. He snatches the sign out of his mouth and holds it up for the family to read.

Immediately, Winston shouts with excitement, "She said yes everyone! Bethany finally said yes! I'm finally going to have a wife!" Uncle Benjamin hands the sign to Amber and then begins to relieve Winston of the rest of the items. Immediately, Winston and Bethany fall into one another's arms and the place erupts with congratulatory cheer and celebration. Mama Netty shouts to the couple above the excitement, "Have you set a date?"

Everyone gets quiet anticipating the answer, and after a long, torturous moment, Bethany begins to explain, "Well, actually..." But Pastor Wynn cuts her off. "Winston, did you bring the documents?" Winston reaches into his inside jacket pocket, pulls out some papers and hands them to Pastor Wynn. Pastor Wynn takes a moment to carefully examine them and hands them to his wife. "Yes, looks like everything is in order. You ready to get started?" More cheer and celebration erupts in the house and everyone gathers around the couple.

After a few minutes, Bethany quiets everyone down to speak. "Who needs a big wedding with all the hoopla?" She looks around the room at each person present before speaking again. "I have what I need for my big day right here and now." She looks at Winston with loving eyes and speaks to the Pastor. "Yes Pastor, we are ready to get started, but first, I would like for us to indulge in Mama Netty's Attitude of Gratitude Thanksgiving tradition that we began on last year." Winston shakes his head in agreement as Pastor Wynn commences to move things along.

"Alright, I think that is most appropriate since this is Thanksgiving Day. Who wants to go first?" Immediately Wendy shoots her hand up in the air as if she is in class and begins to beg to go first. "Oooh, I do, I do...pick me. I'll go first; please, let me go first." Humored, Pastor Wynn reassures Wendy that she can go first. "Alright then; Wendy, it is." "Ah, well... what do I do?" Wendy has a bit of an embarrassed look on her face as she searches for someone to explain the tradition. Amber comes to her friend's rescue. "You just tell us what you're thankful for and why."

Wendy sighs with relief, and immediately begins to rattle off the top of her head the things she's most grateful for. "Oh, that's easy; let's see. I'm thankful for soooo many things, however, today I want to thank the good Lord for my best friend and sister, Amber... who I trust with my life and my secrets and who has been a good example to me. When I got a little off track, you reminded me of what really is important... and I'm thankful. I'm thankful that I listened to your advice because now, I can say ... thank you Lord for my full academic scholarship to the college of my choice which is..."

Amber becomes ecstatic, "No, way... turn up! Duke University!" She turns to give her friend a hug and afterwards, turns to the pastor to plead to be next. "I wanna go next." He nods his head and she proceeds. "Obviously, I'm grateful for my best friend forever. I'm thankful for the bright future we both have and the opportunity to pursue it. David Jr., that includes you too. I'm thankful for my pastors and for them being here today with my family."

She gives them each a sincere look of endearment and speaks directly to them. "You really have made a difference in my life over these past years. I am grateful for my family; we have overcome so much. On today, I'm most thankful for my mother. How fitting is my new baby sister's name... Joy, and that's just what my mother and the rest of this family have found again ... Joy! And for that, I'm forever thankful to God."

David Jr. jumps in to express himself. "For me, what I'm most thankful for on this Thanksgiving Day and every day is that I'm alive and well... and for the love coming from all of those in this room." He hugs his sister, who happens to be standing nearby. Berlene takes the floor next as she looks around the room. "Amen to the love that is in this room. I'm thankful that my sister and I have an extended family in the Clearwater's..."

"Yes", Cherlene quickly agrees with her sister and then adds her own sentiments. "Yes, we're grateful for the love and that we always have a reason to cook huge family meals with all the trimmings on holidays and every special occasion ..." She pauses to clear her throat and then proceeds for a moment of transparency, "Uh, umm...we used to look forward to the entertainment, but — you know — I'm really enjoying the family unity."

Uncle Benjamin speaks in his preacher's voice that no one knew he had. His voice booms through the room. "Behold! How good and how pleasant it is for brethren to dwell together in unity! What a beautiful thing." Then, he speaks in his normal voice to share his gratitude. "I'm most grateful to witness the peace this family is able to enjoy again after so long… Lord knows we have had our share of unrest, but thanks be to God, we have the victory! Amen!"

All the family shout "amen" and afterward a timid Savannah speaks up. "Well, that's what I'm most grateful for today … the victory… I thank God for recovery… I'm not completely there yet, but I thank God for more and more of His grace… His grace gave me my life back… and my sister back… I'm learning that through the grace of God and with family, there's nothing I can't accomplish…"

Bethany takes Savannah's speech as a cue to go next. "… And accomplish, you will, Savannah. I look around today and I can see that this house is so full of love, happiness… smiles… a welcomed contradiction from our past. In this year, I have learned how to put on the attitude of gratitude. Pastor Mary challenged me to write a list of things I could choose to be grateful for. It is a long list that is growing every day. It wasn't until I looked at that list that I was able to let go of the past and truly, from my heart, begin to forgive...and be healed.

What I realized is that I was taking a whole lot of people for granted... my family. I want to thank you for bearing with me when I was unbearable." She turns her attention back to Savannah as she holds Winston's hand. "Savannah, I want to thank you for the sacrifices you have made for me. Because of them, to some degree, I am who I am today." She takes a slight pause in her speech to signify something important is about to be announced and then continues.

"Now, I've already discussed this with Amber, and since she has earned a full academic scholarship, we have agreed to bless you with the college fund I set aside for her. Savannah, for the next four years or for however long it takes, your room and board and all your living expenses are paid for. We want you to focus on recovery and to pick up where you left off... you're going back to school... that is, if you want to ..."

Tears surface in Savannah's eyes. "I'm in shock. I never expected this... of course, I will. Yes, I want... I mean — I do." Mama Netty interrupts, "Speaking of I do's, I would like to say to Bethany, the Bible says that 'two are better than one because they have a good return for their labor' because 'one may be overpowered [but] two can defend themselves' and they can help one another if one falls down. Today, I am thankful for the blessing of marriage. Bethany, Winston... congratulations. I'm happy for you. May you enjoy these good benefits in marriage the way I have with my new husband..."

Berlene and Cherlene begin to serve the Apple Cider Champagne to the family. Mr. Thompson steps over to his wife, takes her hand and begins to speak. "I'll take it from hear, darling. On this Thanksgiving, I'm so ever grateful for the wife that God has given me... Netty, thank you for saying 'I do.' You have made this old man feel like he is alive again..." He puts his attention on the pastors. "Now, I learnt me a little Bible scripture too since I've been married, pastors, and it goes like this... Ecclesiastes 4:11: 'again, if two lie down together, then they have heat, but how can one be warm alone?' No more cold, lonely nights for this old man."

Beaming at Bethany, Winston speaks up. "And no more moments in life spent alone that are worthy to be cherished. I'm thankful for the life God has given me to look forward to. The new family that I am inheriting ... thank you for welcoming me into the family; though, I've felt that I have been a part of this family for a very long time... Bethany, this day has taken a long time coming, and I'm so ever grateful I didn't grow weary in waiting...It's our due time and truly, I have reaped a beautiful harvest. I have loved you for a very long time, my dear...and I look forward to sharing our joy and making moments to be cherished for the rest of our lives."

As Pastor Mary places her hand in her husband's hand, she shares, "Cherished moments! That's what I am most grateful for this Thanksgiving... in marriage, life and in ministry." "Ditto for me, baby." Pastor Wynn lifts his wife's hand up to his lips to kiss it. Afterwards, he looks her in the eyes and speaks directly to her. "I count it an honor to do this life with you by my side." Then, he speaks to all present as he raises his glass and all follows suit. "Here's to God, the Father, who is the giver of life, family, unity, love, happiness and joy... here's to best friends forever and chances to start afresh — to achievements and honor — to huge holiday dinners, and to the cherished moments of life."

They all drink from their glasses. Afterwards, Winston and Bethany make their way to the center of the room where Pastor Wynn is standing. The couple take their places in front of him, Bethany on Winston's left. Uncle Benjamin and David take places next to Winston. Amber makes her way to the kitchen counter where the beautiful bouquet of flowers Winston brought with him lay. She quickly snatches them up and begins to make her way to the bride. Without saying a word and with a huge smile on her face, she presents the makeshift bridle bouquet to her mother. She and Savannah stand a few feet away from Bethany to serve as her bridesmaids.

When all are settled, Pastor Wynn begins. "Dearly beloved, we are gathered together today here in the sight of God and in the face of this company to join together for the union this man, Winston Avalon, and this woman, Bethany Clearwater. Into the holy state of marriage, these two come now to be married."

THE END